D1564610

F

8

THE MAN
WHO WALKED
TO THE MOON

A NOVELLA BY

HOWARD McCORD

MCPHERSON & COMPANY

THE MAN WHO WALKED TO THE MOON

Published by McPherson & Company
Box 1126 Kingston, New York 12402,
with assistance from the Literature Program
of the New York State Council on the Arts.
Designed by Bruce R. McPherson.
Typeset in Baskerville.
Printed on pH neutral paper.
Manufactured in the United States of America.

First paperback edition published 2005.
0-929701-78-X
1 3 5 5 7 9 10 8 6 4 2   2005 2006 2007

The Library of Congress has catalogued
the hardcover edition as follows:

McCord, Howard, 1932-
The man who walked to the Moon : a novella /
by Howard McCord. -- 1st ed.
      p.   cm.
ISBN 0-929701-51-8 (hardcover)
I. Title
PS3563.A263M28   1997   97-15513
      813'.54--dc21

for Jennifer

Whatever flames upon the night
Man's own resinous heart has fed.
                    —W.B.YEATS

THE MAN
WHO WALKED
TO THE MOON

CHAPTER 1

I LEFT STERNS at 4:00 a.m., taking the dry wash north under stars banked heavy and distant in the sky. The bed was sand, gravel, and fist-sized smoothed nodules of granite and gneiss, the sand sides of the arroyo a darker shadow at each side, cutting the stars. For the first half hour I concentrated on my footing, half-stumbling a few times on watermelon rocks working their way toward the town. My pack always feels awkward during the first hour or so of walk, but I can make small adjustments on the straps and belt without pausing, working my shoulders against the load till it settles in, and clear my balance's acceptance of the new geometry without thinking much about it. The sky gradually lightened, and the silhouettes of mesquite and ocotillo mixed with yucca became more distinct. The raw form of The Moon filled a quarter of the skyline before me.

Three days passed in such a way: walk from 4:00 a.m. till after lunch, sometimes late into the afternoon, supper, sleep, and awake again, till The Moon took up half the sky, and the way began to grow steep. I eat very little, and tea or water is my only drink, save for a sip of brandy at sunset. There is little need for shelter as one approaches The Moon, and my camps were the plainest. Water becomes no problem after the fourth day, for The Moon seeps light tears down its slopes in small springs. Higher on The Moon the wind can be an enemy.

It is not uncommon for canyons which appear to open the heart of a mountain to a walker to show resistance once the walker enters in. They narrow, throw down great boulders and raise dry waterfalls, sometimes moss wet in shade, and choke themselves with brush. My canyon was not uncommon, and did these things. Half a day in, I chose to leave the canyon and climb the east ridge, which, though waterless, permits advance, and clarifies the spirit with its view.

The ridge rose steeply for the rest of the day, then leveled as the sun set. I camped a mile farther on, where an outcrop fifty feet high posed its own problem in the growing dark, and a small group of pine offered their music in the air.

My name is Gasper, William Gasper, and I do nothing for a living but live, simply. My family is undistinguished, and my background ordinary. I prefer walking alone to all other steady activities. Doubtless such a vocation reflects a social inadequacy in my personality. However, since I have nothing to contribute to society of much worth, save an icy mind, I can imagine myself only a laborer or small clerk, a servitor as I was to

the military. It has never been of any importance
to me to seek a means by which I might be more
comfortable with others or others with me. I have
walked in many places over the years, happy with
my choice. For the past five years I have walked
The Moon time and again, and no urge has come
in me, as it has in the past, to seek new ground.
The Moon suffices.

I once spent two years in the area around
Mount Silverthrone and Fang Peak, and enjoyed
the sweep of Klinaklini Glacier, but the winters
are bad, and the brush a terrible chore, so I came
south to The Moon, where the way is clear, in its
way.

The night passed, as all my nights do, with
dreams only of where I am. It is as though I possess
some incorporeal eye which functions alone when
I sleep, studying the land about with a dream's
intensity, and which then informs my waking mind
with a greater knowledge of the terrain than I
might suppose was possible. My nights are nearly
always such, and the eye works, and I find my way
by sure anticipation.

This useful content to the night has kept me
hale, though the only dangers walking as I do are
wrong confidence, geology, weather, and those
occasional objects which tumble out of my past, as
unexpected but as natural as the meteors which
pierce the night. More than once I have wakened
before the first visible sign of a squall, followed
my eye's foreseeing, and saved myself from
undue wet or cold. Once such prescience saved

me from a rockfall. This is the pretty explanation I offer myself, though wiser souls might rightly claim there is no eye, but only a mind's sleeping consideration of small signs given the day before, openly, but unnoticed. As with most explanations, it is mainly chatter in the quiet, blackbird-words.

It was colder the next dawn, and after tea I scouted the outcropping and found an easy line up it. I climb hard only when I must, though bouldering in the late afternoon after a day's walk is like a little music, playful and relaxing. The crop ran back like a diminishing chevron on the ridge's sleeve; in two miles I might have skirted it, but lost height, and I do not like that. The ridge increased in steepness beyond, bare of much growth. Trees grow on north slopes and deep in canyons here, not where too much sun sucks up the water. On the northern back of The Moon were miles of ponderosa, aspen higher, juniper below. On the south, low brush, rock, mostly rock. I'd rather walk on good rock than grass, though in the north, tundra of the right sort is like kitten backs.

The Moon is the mountain of nowhere, ignored by those who live within sight of it, as well as by those who, in different times, might be fascinated by its isolation and difficulties. It is not a climber's mountain, nor a hunter's. There are some fine walls in two canyons, and half a dozen crags nearly worth the effort; there's some game. But its charms, like certain women's, are not obvious, and reveal themselves only to an occasional misfit.

You know these mountains of Nevada, or the Steens, perhaps. The Moon, as they do, covers itself with anonymity. It is a vague blue blur from the nearest highway, and one must be as devious as a cat to find any approach closer by car. Horseback or afoot, it's too far for what it seems to offer. It is a perfect mountain for our times, caught partly in an alien dimension, as unintelligible as most good novels, and as effortlessly boring to one who skims topographic maps with an eye to excitement. It is a perfect mountain for William Gasper.

I am William Gasper. And if it seems strange that I repeat my introduction so soon, remember that I am as plain as my cooking, have no friends to speak of, and blend, by practice, into any background. I am something like sea-level: a constant always in turmoil, never quite evident from observation. I move even when I sleep, though my name gives me demarcation. I came to Stern five years ago and persuaded Mary-Gail Henry, who runs the cafe there, to rent me the packing case which rests about one hundred yards behind the cafe. I have no knowledge of its original contents, mining equipment probably, but it now contains those personal effects of mine which I do not carry on my back, some score of magazines which I will eventually bequeath to the fire, and other odds and ends which even a scrupulous person may acquire unawares. I do not sleep in the packing case, having eschewed picturesque romanticism some time past, but I sleep beside it. In the worst weather I pitch my tent, but generally that's a bother. I wash from a pot, and scurry a quarter-mile or so into the desert each morning to take my bowel movement. I piss after a shorter walk. All this, of course, occurs only when I am in residence. But as I told you, my vocation is walking, and Stern sees me no more than a dozen days a year.

How do I eat? The normal way. What you mean is how do I get what I eat. I eat little; my metabolism is happily abstemious, and I am, as are you, of an omnivorous species. But I am without the social conditioning of tastes I know is common to the rest. When I read of the inhabitants of the Danakil or Kalahari, I feel among compatriots: proteins and carbohydrates come in various guises.

I envy the herbivores' ability to digest cellulose, but that is a negligible impediment, given a mind (which I do not doubt). There have been days in which I wished the good Lord, or Whoever-What, had constructed my kidneys so as not to spill so much good water, and, like the kangaroo-rat and certain antelope, to be able to preserve and even metabolize the stuff. But I am what I am, and thankful for it. I have never been ill, or desperate, although that is probably a failing I must encounter eventually. I shall prefer a swift tempest to the body and the kindness of terrible violence, which I have seen take many men. But let that be. I eat what I eat, and there is little meaning in the differences between my diet and yours. My meaning lies in my walking, in my calm, and in The Moon.

By midday I had walked about five miles on the ridge, which had narrowed and steepened. A hawk, minding his ground, had passed overhead silently, and when I turned to look back down the ridge and out over the desert, I could not see Stern, though the hawk could. There was nothing of interest there for either of us, and my debility was not one to be lamented. The ridge was undistinguished save for its view: much talus, thankfully more solid rock, and deepening spaces to either side. Below, to the left, was the canyon I had deserted the day before. The ridge was new. I was growing thirsty, and would have to cut into the mountain in search of water unless I found the old snow bank which my eye had told me clung against the side of a north-facing cliff in a small side canyon. In another mile I had found it, tucked and hidden in a fold of the ridge with some scraggly white bark pine bent and shaped to their staying. In a pocket among the pine I found a nesting spot and decided to stay the night, though it was still early. The ice-heavy snow melted slowly, but tea speaks snow, finally, and the brooding of the leaves in warmth makes home.

I sleep on The Moon in a simple bivvy sack. The drip from the snow bank ceases as soon as night comes, the winds maneuver like switch engines among the outcrops, and whine in the short trees. The brilliance is not in the wind, but the stars. And I, William Gasper, listen.

ᨆ ᨆ ᨆ

There is a man who lives in the packing case out back, says Mary-Gail Henry. But we never see him. He's not there so much I may be wrong to say he lives there. But he rents the place from me. Twelve dollars a month, or maybe it's twelve dollars a year. It's not much of a packing case anyway, and he sleeps outside, I think. He pays each seventeenth of June, the day he came here, five, six years ago. I think he eats grasshoppers, or ants. Maybe both. He doesn't buy meals here. Back when, you ate what you caught and skinned, but he eats them all. Hide, hair, and crackling beetle shell. We ain't seen him for a month or more. But he's not, you know, what you'd call deranged. He's just queer. There's something mean in his eyes sometimes or something cold. Best not mess with him.

〜〜〜

The Moon bends upward as you would expect it to if you were walking it, but differently than you see it afar. The top is snow-free out of some diffidence or crank of weather. Above, nearly all the way up, you'll find snow pack in odd places, never very big. It's like the Wallowas, that way. But a hump, not trills. No Alps, no long green fairways toward the top. Just brute hill gone up, and keeping. I've never found a cave worth speaking of in all its miles. One year I did make a hut like Wittgenstein, two ridges south of where I'm writing. Corbelled stone fit for an Irish monk, but I have no prayers. I stayed about four months there, and marked the rising of a single star on slate, the lines deployed as if they were for fire.

I like sleeping under stone. It's a cat's space,

and how he might sleep, tucked and furled, immune. You don't know small, with things. You don't know smoke, or melted water, or the hardiness of walk.

The south spur of The Moon slices upward in the night, final, sharp, and distinct as the cold wind. It has become like no other mountain. Calm as I would wish to be, am. A shadow taken up substance, solid, real. I slept lightly for a few hours, my eye wandering the slopes, and awoke as the stars' lights began to wane. My eye informed, in its half-remembering way, that another person was somewhere on The Moon, asleep, emitting a presence like a low, guttering candle. I could not fix the location precisely. Somewhere left or right, not above, I thought, more likely below. Whatever sense it was could identify no more clearly than this suggestion. A sleeping gypsy.

I encounter few people willingly, but I am not crippled by them, or fearful. They are a distraction in the landscape, a mild irritant to be avoided generally, but a modest excitement as well, when few or alone. I am not without curiosity about my species, nor a certain crude expertise in dealing with them.

I lay there in the grey darkness and pondered my day's activities. It would be simple to continue on up the ridge, comparatively immune to discovery by the other. Or I might stay the day in camp, hidden as it was, and wait for the next night's voyage by my eye more precisely to locate the traveler. Or again, I might leave my camp in place, and make a few hours' survey of the ridge and canyons below unencumbered with my pack, and discover who it was that wished to walk The Moon this day. I brewed a cup of tea over pine twigs, and made a breakfast with the remaining hot water, dropping four dried apricots in the mixture. I watched the apricots expand slowly, and the sun mesh again with the blue of the sky, deciding. I would continue up the ridge another day, attentive to the world below, in watch for movement, and in night, sleep freely as possible, permitting my eye long voyage. If, on rising, I still sensed the other, I would make a search.

The reasonableness of my decision stirred me to movement, and it was not long after that I broke the crest again, where I paused to study the ridge and canyons with my monocular. I saw no sign of my companion.

By midday, clouds of a summer storm moved across the ridge, obscuring the heights of The Moon. I welcomed them for their very obscurity as well as their freshness. The brief downpour the storm brought provided me with nearly a pint of water, caught on a plastic sheet. Thunder barked and rolled as the clouds swept past. I washed my body in the freshness of the rain, and shivered in the glory. Lustrations for The Moon, and an omen.

I found a level, sheltered spot on the west side of the ridge (which was now running northeast by southwest), and made my camp by rolling out my sleeping bag into the bivouac sack, and doubling it back for a cushion. After a small supper I walked along the ridge until sunset, watching the rising sheet of land below for sign, but only a vague unsettledness in my mind indicated any presence save myself, the mountain, and its customary inhabitants. There was no excitement in this feeling, nor any apprehension. Curiosity remained, and, admittedly, a little irritation. I felt, though without good reason, a proprietary interest in The Moon, and would, if I had the power, have demanded my permission for others to wander upon it. I did not enjoy these thoughts, for I know my own obsession with freedom, and did not know how I might think to deny it to another who did not infringe on my own. A certain amount of inconsistency in my own mind seems normal enough, for we all are tugged back and forth between opposing goods.

My interior life is dry and spare. I am, as far as I know, the last of my kind. My family is extinct, and I will join oblivion in due course. I have no close relationship with any person and am as alone and free as it is possible to be in this world. Mary-Gail Henry collects my rent and saves my mail; we hold infrequent conversations, and I find this satisfactory. I once did a man some service on my way. It was of no consequence to me, though of considerable importance to him, and he subsequently expressed his gratitude with an annuity which exceeds my requirements. It was a gracious gift, and I am not so vain that I would deny its usefulness to my life. It gives me discretion I might otherwise have to struggle for. I lie, for my livelihood was death. Death as a service. Honest service. I do not lie.

∿∿ ∿∿ ∿∿
∿∿ ∿∿ ∿∿

He's as idle as a cassowary, says Mary-Gail Henry, but I haven't anything against him. He claims the big mountain back there as pretty much his own, and I don't know anybody who'd argue that. They don't want it. An idiot might try to raise goats on it, but as far as cattle goes, they don't go that far for that little grass. Old Man Heber was up there once, thinking of leasing some land, but he came back disgusted, and the BLM man don't want no part of it. It's, as they say, part of our national heritage and belongs to the government, but you couldn't suck a teacup of water from all of it, and a cow would die before she got halfway there. And if you could. Just suppose you could get some cattle back there, you'd have to drive them eighty waterless miles to a place a truck could load them, and they'd be dry as sticks and thinner. Just ask Higgins. He tries. No, there's nothing there but there. Ain't no minerals, either, or they'd found them long time ago. One time I thought Mr. Gasper was a prospector, but to tell the truth he don't know galena from feldspar, and the only gold he's ever seen was in a mirror in his mouth. You know why they call it The Moon? Because it's as dead as. About as fertile as cigarette smoke. Just look at the maps. They don't lie, do they? Now if he likes it back there, fine. He don't bother nobody. And if you want to go traipsing out there, too, why, there's no one to stop you. But remember, it's farther than it looks, and twice as mean. And Mr. Gasper, he's picky about his privacy.

∿∿ ∿∿ ∿∿
∿∿ ∿∿ ∿∿

My name is William Gasper, and I have fifty years, half the century allotted me. My mind works as do stars on a cold and feckless night. Under my bunk in the packing case in Sterns, locked and secure in a heavy metal chest, lie the tools of my trade: rifles, pistols, and a shotgun. They are elegant, like silent watchdogs, and lightly used. Each is a swift, efficient machine, beautiful to hold, filled with potential, compassionate. I keep them dry and lightly oiled, and use each only three or four times a year, for I no longer hunt wild game as I did before. On this Moon ramble I carry in my pack a 9mm pistol in case I come to hanker after meat.

I am left-handed, and remember my second grade teacher insisting that my writing paper be positioned on my desk as all the others were, so that I would develop a hook-hand and write illegibly. It was about then that I gave up on school. So it was that Andrew Carnegie's gift to Soledad became my mentor, where the librarians indulged my habit of reading books upside down. After half a dozen experiments standing face to face with a librarian, reading simultaneously with her from the text beneath her eyes, I was not molested further, and indeed became a minor curiosity, called to demonstrate my art from time to time when the afternoon dragged on, and a sympathetic borrower fell into conversation with the librarian while I was there. I read science, technology, history, archeology, the complete *Golden Bough*, and the bad philosophers. Voltaire, Schopenhauer, and

God's beast, Nietzsche, kept me in junior high school, where I missed all the main points, and argued endlessly over the fine ones. In high school, I was worse, except at shooting. I won enough medals shooting that I was passed through Lesser Gibberish and Minor Confabulation as a courtesy to the R.O.T.C.

After that, I moved, in my left-handed way, into the Marine Corps. Again, shooting made straight my way. Marines admire a marksman, no matter how inelegant he may be on parade. I was set to go to Camp Perry in 1950, with talk of a future Olympics, but was called instead to minister to the North Koreans. In high school one must be able, 39 or 40 times out of 40, to hit a circle seventeen one-hundredths of an inch in diameter at fifty feet. So it was I honed my life by small margins, aiming at four hundred out of four hundred. From four positions. It was not a bad way to learn control. The Marines also taught me to jump from airplanes, to strangle with a wire, and to avert my eyes from nothing.

The stranger moved up the mountain during the night. This was either foolhardy or dangerous, and I could not understand why anyone free of some obligation would have done so. It would be tedious, and it excited me. But so my eye reported when I awoke. I could hardly smell the body, hear the lungs' intake and exhalation, feel the blood pounding. There had been no moon, so the walk was by starlight, over broken rock.

I admire a mountain walker as I do a runner—

the solemn selection of the pace, a mesh of aerobic efficiency, muscle tone, stride, and desire.

In Iceland, one of the great runs is to circuit the Hofsjokull, a fine glacier mount which sits just to the west of dead center there. One lap is just about 150 kilometers, and any time under 50 hours is not bad, considering the glacial streams to cross, and the bad footing in the Kerlingarfjoll. It's not a race you are apt to run except against yourself. One great advantage a walker has—his kit goes with him, food and warmth for rest. A runner runs all but naked. When I did the Hofsjokull, I scooped water with my hand, and ate from a 12-ounce bag of Brazil nuts, dried apricots, sesame seeds and raisins, chopped fine, carried in a waist bag, along with two pairs of socks.

This walker had picked a trail by starlight and now, with dawn, I felt her sleeping, protected by an overhanging cliff. I am uncertain about people who choose to walk by night. I admire their skill, but mistrust, suspicion, doubt of their motives rises like a cloud before their faces, and I do not see them clearly. Why follow me? Why even know of me to follow? And a woman? For by this time I had noticed that every hidden announcement of her presence was couched in the feminine. The pronouns were 'she' and 'her,' as though the wind had carried a trace of her woman's musk to me. I thought of my hand gliding into her wetness, the soft prickle of hair on my palm, and the cushion of her mound. I had not been with a woman for a long time now, and had seldom thought on the matter. I felt a small smile tug at my cheek, under the whiskers. Perhaps when we met, we would fuck on the summit, and groan like the wind gone mad.

Yes, William Gasper wears a beard, and has for a decade. It requires no vow to be so faithful, simply an aversion to shaving, as faithfulness of any kind can simply be rejection of the opposite. It is not that I find skepticism so appealing, as belief so lacking in dignity. I too would as lief pray with Kit Smart as any man, but only because he was so touchingly mad, and a grand poet. I would howl to the moon with him, if he asked.

The dawn was full now and I stirred myself to heat water for tea. I let the tea steep in the cup while I mixed the rest of the hot water with some soy gruel, and dropped some raisins in. Soy powder is a fine blessing, though it makes you fart. But it is light in weight, and most nutritious. It is my protein base, to which I add thankfully any leaping, crawling, or scuttling delicacy I happen on. I thought this morning of grouse, usually common at this elevation, and pathetically eager to be eaten. Or perhaps a marmot for supper. The grouse I could get with a rock, but the wily marmot would require a stalk, and use of my pistol. Perhaps for supper. Perhaps.

But supper was at the nether end of the day, and not to be considered now. I sluiced some tea through my mouth, gritted the tannin between my teeth, and thought of resin. The bag puffs white at a slap, and I could approach the bar, clean it, double bodyweight, and pause for the jerk, or I could lift my arms, leap to the bar, swing, raise my legs, kick, and in that marvelous articulation called a kipp, mount the horizontal bar. I think I have more kinesthetic memories than visual ones, but seldom dream them. I wonder what a dancer dreams? Is it the paradigms of movement, the resin dust on the feet, the slap, the twist and stop, the sweat? I held the cup to my lips while my mind wandered over resinous things, gently exhaled, and watched the steam drift out toward the distant desert. I could see Sterns, ninety miles away, or where it was, where I knew it was. Somewhere below me, the woman stirred in her sleep, and moved her arm across her face to keep away the light. She would sleep till noon or better.

The raisins in my gruel had softened now, and I contemplated their flaccid bodies with my tongue as I finished breakfast. Long ago I had carried texts with me on my walks, some poet, the fragments of a philosopher, gossip and the like. But such matters no longer interest me. The tongue licking the mustache after a sip of tea holds as much wisdom as a distich by Herakleitus. There was a time when I was charmed by the truculence of Edward Dahlberg, and even went so far as to write in his mode the beginnings of a spiritual autobiography which I called "The Vision of Rumplestiltskin." But I sold his books, finally, as I sold all my books, finally, and find him as meaningful and poignant as the stick of tannin to my teeth after tea, but not more so. Memory is as useful as a text, and as treacherous, though it cannot be escaped so easily, or sold. I come to terms with mine by making few demands of it, and not caring to correct it. What it presents, let be. Who can know otherwise anyway? My days are spent in play with the present, which is my true delight. The moment perceived, and the body's instant response, whether to yawn or leap. Doubtless it required some years of instruction from the past, some active use of texts and memory to create the capability of reasonable response, but once done it can be forgotten as easily as any schooling. The process of learning is irrelevant, once the learning is done. There is no particular point, when speaking a foreign language, to dwell on details remembered of the classroom, the teacher's skewed smile, or the fine leg of Lenore Walters, across the aisle. Speak, and get on with it. (Yet my memory is as precise as a data bank.)

I slid out of my sleeping bag, and the cool morning wind at eleven thousand feet put chillbumps on my thighs as I pulled my pants on. I sat on the bag, laced up my boots, rose, then stuffed the bag in its sack, folded the bivy sack, and readied my pack. The gruel cup I hung on my belt, aiming to wash it at the next water, up the ridge a mile or so, and left around a corner of rock. The day was pure, and the spring flowers here on the ridge whipped back and forth as though jerked by hidden strings. I wiggled my toes into a fit of socks and boots, swung the pack up, and began another day of walking on The Moon.

I am not to be held, says Gail Henry, accountable for anybody's presence or absence, including my own. Mr. Gasper is a gentleman of means, although not an awful lot, and how I don't know. But means he has got. He don't mess with anybody, and I see no call for anybody to mess with him. I don't think you'd get away with it. You know, the Spanish call their bachelors solteros, "solitaries," and that pretty well describes him. He is as solitary a creature as I have ever come across, and out here you see some mighty peculiar ones. I knowed a man what milked snakes once, I knowed another what claimed to have killed maybe six people here and there, all of them deserving it, according to him, and why not? There's that many around in most folk's lives. And another that just shook a lot, never talked much, just shook, and didn't want to say why. Well, in that bunch Mr. Gasper shines like a saint of reasonableness, and maybe in another he wouldn't. He comes and goes, mostly goes. And like I told you, he's out there somewhere and it's his business and not mine and not yours. Now his packing case is locked with a padlock, and I just checked. I don't want you fooling around out there for that's my property, and I took down your license number just in case. So let us get on decent footing, not bother each other, stop talking about Mr. Gasper, and maybe have a cup of coffee. You are polite enough, but you have to admit you have been pushing things a bit. And I'm not to be pushed. Leave a note. I'll see he gets it whenever he gets back.

~~~ ~~~ ~~~

I am doubtless empty-headed, but I am not giddy. Nothing of any great importance passes through my mind, nor has it ever. If there are profound thoughts in this universe, I have not thought them. I keep to the task of the moment, and at this moment my task was to walk a ridge to water, wash my gruel cup, and fill my belly and my bottle with water. The seep, for it was more that than spring, was formed by run-off channeled into a fissure, a deep V of cliffs. The cliffs faced south, and so caught the warmth of the sun. There was always a bit more greenery there than elsewhere hereabouts, and I had often camped there. I had dug out a small basin in the soil, and a liter or two of water generally sat there waiting. Last time here, perhaps two months ago, still in the cold time, I found bear scats, from some early waking, wide ranging boar, and the water frozen.

The ridge was steep, but I stuck to the crest. I will slip into the low gear of switchbacks on a bad slope only when I am forced to by fatigue or curiosity. My natural inclination is toward the diretissima. My face began to warm, both from the sun and the exertion, and I began to hum. Humming is the sign of the truly asocial man, for no other sound is at once so soothing and pleasant to its maker and so irritating to any other listener. I hummed until I reached the line of cliffs where the spring was found, and turned along its base. Approaching water anywhere one should keep silence, for water attracts many things. I moved carefully and correctly, for there was sign at the spring: the impress of a sleeper last night, bootprints just dry of the morning dew.

I stepped in close to the cliff and slowly scanned the ridge and the cliffs for my new companion. I saw nothing, and after a few moments I returned my gaze to the sleeping place. The impress of one body in a sleeping bag was clear, and there on the right side, near the head, was a deeper impression, where my left-handed friend had leaned on his right elbow while heating water over his Primus. The boot marks were about my own size, elevens. They seemed to head to the right, along the cliff base, but the ground was too rough for trailing. I had little doubt I would encounter the traveler during the day.

I returned to the crest of the ridge, watered and curious. As I climbed, my mind played with the evidence of presence. My eye had told me nothing of the traveler above me on The Moon. It reported only of the woman below, still undetected by my more conventional senses. My eye, my feelings, told me nothing. I could not detect the slightest tremor of apprehension, the least twinge of suspicion. Whoever had slept the night so close by was harmless. Or so my feelings told me. My mind always questions my feelings. The woman below might be a figment of my imagination. But someone fully solid had slept at the seep last night. Someone was quiet and inconspicuous.

The wind at my back picked up, and there was the smell of rain in the air. To the west, some early summer cumulus mounted up and darkened, and I knew that soon I would have some lightning to watch. And there is no grander display in nature, unless it be the aurora.

Many years ago near Ruidoso, New Mexico, my mother witnessed an appearance of ball lightning, and one of my dearer wishes has been to witness it as well. It was summer, and a storm whipped up in the afternoon over the peaks, rain pelted down, and then, in front of her some hundred yards, a lightning bolt struck a Ponderosa pine. The instant the discharge hit the tree, it formed itself into a ball about thirty inches in diameter and began to roll slowly down the pine, seeming to rotate as it moved. It rolled down to the base of the tree, paused a moment at the ground, and then began to roll along the ground toward her. After it had traveled about fifty yards, it vanished.

I heard another story from my mother's uncle, who lived some fifty miles to the southeast. This happened in the late thirties. A summer thunderstorm, a lightning bolt (or thunder overhead), and a ball of lightning floated through the window of the kitchen, moved across the room, went through the door into the living room, into the fireplace, and disappeared up the chimney. Three people witnessed it. I should like to see something like that, and I court thunderstorms for the chance. I have seen sheet lightning, and I saw the crown flash the very time it was first described for science by Gall and Graves, being a little north of Ann Arbor that day, on a peculiar errand. I did not know what it was until I saw the pages of *Nature* a year later, and made the connection. I remember the thunderhead crowned by a bright ring of radiance pulsing upward. It caused a great yearning in me for the mountains of the west.

When I am away from the mountains, I grow cross, and my dreams are populated by baleful images of prairie, or the suppuration of architecture. I can hardly sleep in my packing case any longer, and long gave up a tent for my wanderings except in the foulest of climes. I do not easily accede to a barrier between me and the infinite curve of the universe above. I have slept in caves with some gladness, but only for short periods. They seem kin to my bivy sack. Some old memory of troglodyte or troll lingers in my blood, but my gods are fundamentally those of the sky, however profoundly otiose.

I kept my pace on the ridge, as it had leveled out a bit, and I had a long stretch of easy grade before me. The western sky continued to boil and darken, but the clouds were still miles away, and I did not expect rain until afternoon. The wind on the ridge was brisk and chill, but the wind on the ridge is always so. The cliffs on the southern face below me fell away steeper and longer, bending to the northeast as they formed the west wall of one of The Moon's finer canyons. The ridge at the spot where I now stood was 12,500 feet in altitude. The summit of The Moon was only about 2000 feet higher, though still some miles away. All morning long, no matter where my mind wandered, my eyes had kept alert for a moving figure. There had been none. There had not even been the nervous circling of a hawk in the canyon below. I decided I would not concern myself overmuch about the nature of my brother's business, or his present whereabouts. But I did believe I should keep alert enough not to be surprised.

It was the apricot at lunch that signaled the answer. A plump, lush California apricot, dried to perfection. I thought of the Mediterranean, orchards, white, white stone, figs, the palace at Mycenae, the old times, when women ruled more openly. It was Cerridwen, of course, and the Palug cat. The cat that curses. She had sent him on before her, she of the white face, he of the black, a "slender cat reclining on a chair of old silver." Pasht with a brogue, but big as a plough ox. Well, the old sow could follow me as she wished, and send her cat anywhere. I have slept among snakes before, and soundly.

The apricot was good, and I had three more halves as I thought out the patterns. I had found a comfortable outcropping on the ridge which made a small protected alcove, so that the wind bubbled harmlessly by at the sides. The noon sun was strong, and I could feel the extra ultra violet rays at the altitude on my cheeks, while the western clouds grew taller and more filled with energy. The thunderheads were probably pushing 50,000 feet. Years ago, crossing the Pacific, I had flown in a C-54 in a shipment of madmen through the most glorious thunderheads I have ever seen. It was sunset, perhaps 200 miles west of the California coast, after a long day's flying. The pilot threaded his way through them like a cat slithering through a bamboo grove. With each turn, new lights, new shadows, new colors boomed through the window. Years later, flying up the Ganges valley during monsoon, I had witnessed a similar beauty, against the backdrop of the Himalayas. A DC-3, that time. Royal Nepal Airlines.

I began accounting of a time in my life then, caught by the tug of weather memory, the skies of southern India, the dusty white of Greece and the grey-black distance of the snow peaks in Nepal. Weather signs that turned to some interior light sifting through crevices in my past. I both remember well, and am haunted by the suspicion that it is all fabrication, that if I were really put to it, nearly all my days would prove specious, and I as empty of a past as a rock. It is as simple as this: what I remember may not have happened. And with all my past goes me. A man without family or friends, a solitary, one who seldom encounters others, may come to disbelieve his own existence in most of the usual ways. Are we not defined in large part by our relationships with others, confirmed in life by the witness of others? If Mary-Gail Henry, for example, did not see me for months, for years, might I not effectively cease to exist? I would be a memory, and memory is a trap. And what would I have to say in the matter, speaking to no one? It would be easy to come to believe that I had never been, and whatever it was that was creating this disturbance of consciousness was no more than a dust devil of sorts, a spinning of the wind, now lost and gone. So if it were Cerridwen and the Palug cat, ready to throttle me into the past, it would be no more a gesture than I make, putting on my coat. Or a willow bending to the sun at a burst of wind. I enjoyed this reverie on my diaphanous state, my total fragility, the life and times of a mote. My pack had grown lighter, and my humming magnificent. I came to a point where the cliffs below fell away right at my feet, the ridge narrowing sharply. The noon sun shone into the depths of the canyon, 2000 feet below. I pulled out my monocular and scanned the small area where I knew a small spring worked all year. There was a human figure leaning against a boulder some dozen feet from the spring, a light pack on the ground beside, and a rifle leaning against the boulder, close to the figure's right.

The rifle encouraged me, for it changed the odds. A rifleman loves skylines, two hundred yards, the prone position, hates brush and tight quarters, and night. Most of the confusions of a general can be worked on a rifleman, fewer on a pistolero, and none at all on the poor fiend with a knife. A rifleman imagines a certain sort of ambush, a certain defensive stance, and will make his route accordingly. It is impossible for a rifleman to run any distance effectively. His advantages are a longer sight radius, and so a steadier sight picture, longer range, and generally greater power. But he can use these only if his adversary permits him to. It is hard for him to be quick.

I eased myself into a comfortable and inconspicuous position, and studied the figure. An 8 × 24 monocular and fifty-year-old eyes do not equal one eagle, but I saw what I could. The rifle appeared to be scoped, but I was not certain because of the shadows. The figure's dress was bulky enough, seated, that I could not tell if it were man or woman. I opted for the Palug here, cutting sign for Cerridwen. The figure was at lunch, relaxed, and so I dug out a few raisins and waited. Brown parka, dark green pants, a watch cap, and very quiet. In a few minutes, the figure arose, and I saw the white of a face slowly scan the ridge behind me, and study the line of the cliffs below. Then, with a deliberation I could approve of, the figure swung up the pack, and slung the rifle on his right shoulder. It was scoped. And it was doubtless the person who had slept at the seep, a left-handed rifleman who knew the country well enough to find two waters in half a day, but who worked contrary to right reason. I could see no advantage in moving from the ridge seep to the canyon. It had meant a descent of a thousand feet, and if the canyon were followed through, as it must be unless the figure were a gifted rock climber (and not even one of those, with a rifle), that would place him back on the ridge, after greater trouble than following it. I had walked that canyon a time or two. The going would get quite rough as it tightened up, and the cliffs tumbled together at its nexus. Perhaps the figure meant to climb the next ridge opposite. But why change ridges in the middle of a mountain? I had done so in the past, of course, but I am not always reasonable in the mountains, for I wander,

wander. The figure below trudged up the canyon, staying in the watercourse, moving nimbly across the smooth boulders. It was a good gait, and bespoke some skill. I kept below the skyline and continued up the ridge, checking on the figure below from time to time. After about two miles, the canyon narrowed sharply, and the figure was faced with a choice: to the right, not at all; ahead, with difficulty; to the left, last chance. The ridge to the east demanded a hard scramble over talus slopes and short outbreaks of cliffs. The route to the canyon head was steep and tumbled, and led to a demanding climb for someone with a rifle and pack, a 5.4 or so. The cliffs below me were for serious climbers only, and approached the Gunnison in difficulty. It was ahead, or east. The figure paused, but only shortly, and then began working up the talus slope to the east.

My family, as I said earlier, is undistinguished. We have always provided America with its enlisted men. There's not an officer among them. And we have been here long enough that there have been relatives on both sides of all the wars we've ever been in, locally. Revolutionary and Loyalist, North and South, and as far as I know, some fascist pig on the lately entered German side. Mostly Celt, and the rest Saxon, or a later-sprung Kraut. It is easiest to have illusions about the Celts, in spite of the evidence. One pigheaded, another a dolt, the rest blathering. I know nothing about them, except they came to this country, exiles and losers, and met something that at least kept them occupied. The patronymics went to New York and stayed there, save for a few wild hearts, and the rest scuttled through the Blue Mountains, on to Missouri, and thence to Texas, New Mexico, and places west. I am a Texian, born there of stock so located during Republic times. Comanches scalped and killed my great-great grandmother and her daughter on 5 December 1864, which drove their daddy crazy. I am his son by some remove, and share his craziness. I like to kill the guilty, and am good at it.

The Palug cat had hit a patch of scree and was messing his way upward, like the frog in the well. There's nothing so aggravating as a scree slope. You work for three times what you get. He was a determined cat, however, and I watched him take most of an hour to make a thousand feet. The clouds were boiling on our tails by then and the first lightning strokes were beginning to snap on the ridge.

The wind began to puff up over my back, and the rain began to pelt, so I pulled the hood of my parka up, tightened the apertures (as Ed Sanders might say) and began to look for a place to sit out the passage of this low. Ozone and negative ions are as good, nearly, as bourbon, at least at this altitude, and I was feeling a little wild. I would tell you the safe procedure to avoid lightning strikes while on an exposed ridge, but I see no reason you should not learn it as I did. If you get tweaked by God's long electric finger, I can hardly be to blame. You are a fat-assed nerd anyway, without a pistol within reach, and incapable of running more than three miles without the last rites. You, fart-brain, are a reader, and the only thing I despise more is a writer, who simply ought to announce himself a public masturbator and be done with it. But I am telling my story, you are listening, and so we have a truce, if not respect. I am a writer, you a reader, and if there were a God, he might be amused to have mercy on our souls. Or piss on them. In long electric streaks.

I once had a .45-70 Sharps, and shot a grand bear with it. It makes a noise like artillery without being a Magnum, which is something sophisticated and impure. The .45-70 emits a deep noise, like the soul of a boulder taking leave, or the aspiration of a brontosaurus, pure, simple, rolling, as though someone delivered a telephone pole to your front porch, butt end first. Deep and solid. So was the first lightning strike.

During electrical storms the air is charged with static electricity, and stranger things than we can explain can happen. Colors may effloresce in the strokes which are never seen otherwise, and a strike to the brain doubtless illuminates just as it annihilates. It was such a storm, and I felt the spaces underneath my fingernails as caverns, and the wind through my eyebrows as a groaning, soughing tidal rapture through sequoias. It was a storm in which perspective could easily be lost, or misapplied. At one point I had to grab the rock in front of me to keep from being blown into the canyon below. And after one particular lightning strike I sat quite numb and stupid for minutes on end, as though suspended in some great temporal trough, like an Egyptian king (or better, the servant of a king) resined, tarred and spiced to perduration. It was like going to a bad movie when one hates the idea of a movie anyway.

The Sharps was a blustering big gun, and I wished I had one again. It was a machete among rifles, a D-7 through the brush, an air strike, and I would like to shoot at the clouds, however foolish (you may here choose any adjective, but frivolity will lead you astray from the story) it may seem. Two hundred yards. You can blast whatever in two hundred yards. Beyond that, go to something else. But to two hundred yards you can make any land wanderer on this continent lie down and think about its trespasses. Even the sinless will pretend sin if forgiveness is in the offing.

You see, guns are important because they kill people and other animals. They make certain machines stop. And they are highly selective. They hit whom they are aimed at. If I took a three-foot half-inch reinforcing rod and with all my force brought it down upon your chest and penetrated your whole body in one thrust, I would do far less damage than one .22 Long Rifle hollow point fired at 25 feet, or 25 yards. You would be spitted, sick, and if I hit anything important, dead. But if I didn't, you would have a good chance of recovery. You would have less chance with the .22. Less still with the .38, less with the .357, less with the .45, less with the .44 magnum, and then we have to begin thinking about the trauma a rifle cartridge might cause. Certain high velocity bullets would hit your chest cavity and nearly explode. (Nearly is a very exact word here.) You weigh about as much as a whitetail deer, and can figure the damage by using them as surrogates. Any bullet from .22 LR up can kill with one shot. You will bless the hunter who hits you with something more than 1800 foot-pounds of muzzle energy and more than 2500 feet per second muzzle velocity with more than 100 grains of lead and jacket. Else you will hurt simply, and not be dead so quick. Being dead quick is something our culture has little to say about, as it is given to respirators and the like. If you are going to kill rationally, you have to know how best, why, and more. But if dead you are going to be, quicker is better. That's hunting ethics.

This begins an essay on the snuff. (And I, who could well have been the second gunman, the man on the grassy knoll, will be the lector. I, whose existence is merely suspected.)

~~~ ~~~ ~~~
~~~ ~~~ ~~~

Well, says Mary-Gail Henry, I don't know what has prompted such attention, but you are the third person in as many days to come bothering about poor Mr. Gasper. I gave the others pretty short shrift, and I don't see why I shouldn't you either. He hasn't done anything, because he's not where you can do anything. I mean, when it's you and a mountain, what the hell sort of crime can you commit? And he damn sure doesn't do anything around here. Why, I have a hard time getting him to drink an Orange Nehi, much less sip whisky with me over the kitchen table. And it's store-bought whisky, too. We don't moonshine out here. Never was profitable. Too easy to get the stuff from Mexico, even during Prohibition, and this here state has never had much of that. You know, we got legal whorehouses. Now why don't you go investigate that? I'll tell you, because you'd get about as far as the nearest judge, and those folks with money would have you patrolling the dog runs in Tijuana before you could spit. You don't mess with money. Rule one of any government. And as you is a hireling, well, it follows likewise. No, you and the tax boys come messing with ordinary folk, giving them a hard time, making your quota, till some day there comes a hanging-time, and then we'll see if you're so hot for them rat asses in Washington. Don't wiggle your fingers in the air to shush me, boy, because I don't shush easy. Now I suppose you have a badge or something I could buy in any pawn shop in Las Vegas to impress me with the importance of your presence? Well, show it to me and I'll see if it's your likeness. Well, what the hell, government boy, looks like your little ID done slipped from my fingers into that there pot of boiling eggs and it is puckering up something awful. I just couldn't see if that was your face or not, so you better go back to Washington and get another one and maybe next time you won't be so dumb or I won't be here or they will send you out to investigate Billy Carter or Truman Capote. They both needs it, I'm sure. And tell them folks how an old lady boiled your badge. Ha!

∼∼ ∼∼ ∼∼
∼∼ ∼∼ ∼∼

The dramatics of the storm soon shifted, and I pulled my head back into the hood of my parka to look across the spaces. The lightning went on elsewhere, and the rain steadied to a regular pelt. And then that, too, eased, and small shafts of sunshine began to be visible on the slopes below. In another twenty minutes the wind had softened, the rain ceased, and I was standing, stretching my legs. Storms are crazy things, and often I feel as though I am so caught up in them and their wildness that I go a little crazy. I was shouting with the lightning bolts there, and beginning to dance inside. I guess, to a mountain man, it's a bit like getting drunk, to a sailor. I took off my parka and shook the rain from it, checked my pack, and pulled the SIG P210 from its case rolled in my sweater. It was a darker blue than the darkening sky, and as pure. It is Swiss, and the Rolex of 9mm pistols, as accurate as a specialized target pistol, but clean, slick. I am always reminded of Rilke's panther when I hold it. It understands the breaking of silence. I was still deafened by the thunder and a bit trembly. I pulled the slide back and checked the round in the chamber, then checked the magazine. I had deepened my hip pocket and lined it with chamois. The pistol fit perfectly.

A good pistol is perfect, anyway, unless it has been abused. One of my other delights is a wild old Colt 1911 from well before the Second World War, with the old blueing, not the parker-ized finish. It is lustrous, heavy and dark, and the abyss of its barrel is a glimpse of eternity. I know its history, the lives it took, and the life it repeatedly saved. It is a solace to the hand, and to my machinist's eyes; its weight on my thigh is more welcome than a woman's palm, and the knowledge it is under my pillow more securing than the praises of angels. A pistol is like a Turkoman's prayer beads, and more precise in its grasp of paradise. I came to love the Army .45 as a lad. It was the handgun of Marine heroes in war movies, and of the more muscular Hollywood gangsters, or at least the more ham-handed. It is not a pistol for small hands, though mine are relatively small, and I had to learn to compensate by strength. It is astonishingly accurate, and it fits together like an open puzzle. My love began when I learned to fieldstrip it, and I was quick to disassemble and reassemble with my eyes closed in less than 60 seconds. On such small matters most love affairs begin.

It took a few minutes' work with the monocular to spot the Palug cat, still working the scree slope across the canyon. He had sat out the storm, too, and doubtless had his own reveries. As for the Hag, I would wait till night, when I might go investigating. I moved carefully back over the ridge, where Palug might not observe my route, and pushed with renewed vigor upward. I might have a surprise for both in a few hours.

CHAPTER 2

THE WEST RIDGE I traveled ran east another mile and then, in a gentle arc, turned north, and the cliffs that had once a southern exposure now faced east and the canyon floor was in shadow. The Palug had made his ridge now, where it, too, turned north and joined mine in three miles or so. But it posed a harder route, for four bands of cliffs transversed it like giant steps, each one a hundred or two hundred feet tall. They were not difficult climbs, but each one took thought and time. If I wished, I could reach the juncture of the ridges, and descend the Palug's ridge and meet him just about as he topped the third set of cliffs. My descent would be easily hidden, for the cliffs blocked his view. This could be entertainment, and by night I might have a friend to share brandy with, or another corpse. Days on The Moon are generally less exciting than this, and my persistent humming soon turned into a whistle. I was not as good as Wittgenstein, but I managed a little Mahler, and some Barbados back-street ditties.

Now the Palug cat was a savage kitten, gift of Cerridwen to the people of Arvon, which grew up to be one of the Three Plagues of Anglesey. Why the sow-goddess gave such gifts is of course unknown, but there has hardly ever been a thoughtful deity that did not hand out trouble as easily, or even more easily, than it bestowed blessings. Cerridwen has a nature as given to harm as to good, and I'm not the one to question it. I have received both favors from her in the past, and will again, I suppose. I do not ask. My skill is in recognition, and she knows this. That's why she tried the Palug cat. But every missionary bears the stamp of his god. And I know her white, drawn face as well as I know the dawn. And I know her violence. She learned her trade as a goddess in rough times—when the bones of a child freshly killed might be ground into the wheat as reasonably as our own lights lead us to saturation bombings. I give due deference to the old sow, and she knows it. But that doesn't mean she wouldn't smile to see me spitted.

Here on The Moon I can go a long time without thinking of her or the others. They have their ways of finding me, or anyone they seek. But it's more trouble here, and so I am generally left alone. Perhaps I am again, and the Palug cat simply my suspicion, nothing but a wayfaring stranger, one of those backpackers I read about. Many things are possible in the course of a single day. Each instant is a forest of choices. Mine, the sow's, even yours.

If you are concerned with verisimilitude and probity, know well I have not made myself a gift to paranoia's delusions, nor am I given to quaint expression. Cerridwen is as real as ball lightning, about as explicable, and, in these times, less frequently observed. A single encounter authenticates her existence, even to the most sublimely skeptical. I think there are no ghosts in this universe, nothing supernatural at all. But nature contains enough anomalies to stock all the heavens and hells men have to deal with.

A physicist noted recently that we are able to detect only ten per cent or so of the stuff we know must make up the universe. That is, ninety per cent of the universe is completely unknown. And our science, based on a rough knowledge of how that ten per cent behaves, may be totally inadequate to describe the remainder. That's where I put Cerridwen and her ilk, among the remainder.

I call her the name she called herself when I first encountered her. She liked the sound of Welsh, and she had been pleased by the people, so she used the name. I do not know what she is except part of that remainder. She appears as a woman or animal generally, with extraordinary powers. Certainly the idea of the gods, and of witches, came from man's encounters with her and the others. Combine one real experience, however garbled in the retellings, with fear and ignorance, cupidity, and a desire for power, and you have the history of all religions and such writ cold. Every few years she shows up, scares the shit out of me, damn near kills me, and then goes away. I'm still alive, and for a while I thought she meant only to frighten. But I have decided she is in earnest, and unless I respond with all the urgency a true threat of death poses, she will snuff me without hesitation. I do not know if I have any chance of winning at all. I may have only the chance of postponing the end of the game a while.

So far, she has been sporting and employed no unseemly powers. She will not exact anything more from me than would a most cunning and able human adversary. This is my fourth encounter with her, and my third contest. I hope she finds me entertaining enough to warrant a fifth.

My ridge was nearly level now, and I quickened my pace. I kept below the crest, and headed for a little outcrop a quarter mile away. It wasn't much larger than a house, and at one corner a sharp overhang provided decent protection from most rain and wind. I slipped the pack from my shoulders and leaned it against the dry wall. I filled one parka pocket with gorp, slipped the brandy flask in the other, checked my belt knife and the pistol, and was on my way. I could get along for a day or two without anything else, and I certainly could move faster.

The rain clouds were miles away now, thundering and spilling on the northeast flank of The Moon and the high desert foothills beyond. The sun was bright and the air charged with freshness as I hurried north to the meeting of the ridges. I left the Palug cat to his own devices and concentrated on speed. He had the four great steps to climb and would be busy enough. Twenty minutes after ditching my pack I was on the Palug's ridge, beginning to work my way toward him.

There is really no cover in the Hudson Zone except that provided by geology. The vegetation is ankle-high at best, though the tiny flowers are the most charming of earth's. And the mosses, the worts, the saxifrage, can so bind a hill together that astonishingly steep slopes are possible. I have climbed slopes that were as tidy as a golf green, but stood nigh on edge, and I could have front-pointed them had I been wearing crampons. The Palug's ridge had some sections so inclined. It was altogether a worse choice than mine, and I wondered what stratagem had carried him from a night's sleeping spot on my ridge, down an easy way to the canyon, but up a wearisome scree slope, and then four bands of cliffs, and several long steep rises. It was not mountain sense, certainly, nor a bushwhacker's tactic. I could not doubt that he knew of my presence on the ridge. Not if he was the Palug. But now he had let me gain the heights above him, an advantage I would use. There was no way he could run my flanks, for from his point upwards, the ridge fell away in cliffs on either side. If up the ridge he must, then he must travel a strait passage, not more than a quarter mile anywhere, and generally under two hundred yards.

Such are the thoughts I had as I moved down his ridge, letting the folds of the earth hide me as they would. I, William Gasper, am no stranger to hiding in open places, who once stood within the fold of a crowd and helped create a long, twisted dream. If you learn to hunt caribou and white bear on the Great Barrens, you learn to make the only tree in a thousand miles evaporate at a glance. You come to know when eyes are on you, how never to be skylighted, and how to freeze. You learn the precise moment to kill.

I remember in reading Tolkien the only thing I wanted was an elfin cloak, light, warm, and near invisible. My own parka had been chosen neither so dark nor so light as to be easily seen, and I had put shiny things behind me as a babe. My beard broke the reflective sheen of my face, and I wore no glasses. But the real secret to not being seen are moments of stillness. The eye catches regular movement most easily, erratic movement with difficulty, and stillness with greater difficulty yet. So it is fast when protected, then slow, coupled with still, when exposed, and always quiet.

It was because I was an accomplished stalker and a producing sniper that I first met Cerridwen, and did not spend some years in a North Korean prison camp, or die in the snow. It was December, 1950, bitterly cold. I was just eighteen, a Marine private on a reconnaissance patrol south of Majon. There, as everywhere in Korea, the hills sweep in a confusion of ridges, and my squad, scouting in advance of our company, was working across a ridge by the light of the moon, bright enough on the snow for fast travel. The Chinese were chasing all our asses south still, after the fearsome retreat from Chosin Reservoir. We were looking for an escape route that everyone knew did not exist, but which must be searched for anyway, like religious truth. I don't think our company commander expected ever to see us again. He didn't, as a matter of fact. My squad was down to four men, and we were sent out wearing the last white parka covers available. I had layered sweaters under my field jacket, and had on three pairs of long johns. I remember I had a pair of combat boots two sizes too big, which enabled me to wear three pairs of heavy socks, an indescribable blessing, for this was the winter of frozen feet. It was cold and scary, and we all hoped we would not run into a company of Chinese reconnoiterers complete with an insane bugler. We did, of course, but we had the high ground, and surprise, and so we got away before they could re-group.

What saved us was an incredible little storm which seemed to churn up out of the ground itself. It threw snow so thickly in the air in front of us that we were able to beat back on the ridge, cross to an adjoining one and disappear before the Chinese could find us. From the ridge we could watch the swirling snow, piling up in the bright moonlight like a tower of ice crystals. It covered a square mile like a stationary cyclone, while all around the stars were bright, bitter lights in the night. I don't know if the Chinese company ever emerged from the storm. It looked as though they might well have been buried, or suffocated. Whatever, we were cut off from our company. A burst of Chinese machine pistol fire had taken our radio, and since we could no longer report what we knew we could not find anyway, we decided to find our way back out, wherever that might be.

The moon set about 3:00 a.m., and we could no longer travel. We gathered in close in a little gully, as out of the wind as we could find, split the watch, and hunkered down for a stay. We dug something of a snow cave and managed to heat a canteen cup of water on a fuel tab and make some instant coffee. The radio man discovered his feet had frozen. He couldn't feel anything much below the knee, as he demonstrated with his pocket knife in a sad, hysterical gesture. His name was Guilfoy. The coffee was no help for him. When we started out at dawn, he kept up for a while, then began to fall into the snow. We'd help him back up, and boost him on. Then one time he fell down and it was obvious he was dead. It set the tone for the day. We were moving very slowly through deep snow, following a high ridge. We were sure the valleys below were filled with Chinese and North Koreans. We could see them sometimes. Maybe they even saw us, but they couldn't reach us. The pillar of snow dominated my thoughts when I had any, but most of the day I did not think, I responded like a raw nerve. By night two others were gone. I had enough sense left to dig a little cave in a snow bank and try to survive. I insulated myself pretty well, and decided to concentrate on eating and keeping warm. I had suggested that we stop earlier, but the other two noted correctly that the longer we waited, the farther we would have to go to catch up with our retreating troops. I agreed with that, and kept going till I was the majority. I didn't think I'd ever catch up, and if I wanted to stay alive, I should keep from freezing right now, and not later. So the cave. I stayed there about thirty-six hours, ate all but one of the K rations, and made a plan.

My frozen comrades had been right. It was a bad choice to try to catch a retreating army itself being chased by six million Chinese. It might make more sense to cut east, right to the Korean coast, steal a boat, and try to make it south by sea. I would have to be very careful in crossing the valleys, but I had no more than twelve miles to go, and the Chinese would not be looking too carefully for movement to the east. Their concentration was southward. Whatever, I had damn few options.

I left at dark, and prayed for enough clouds to make it hard for anyone to see me, but enough moonlight at the right time that I could see my way. When I crossed the first valley, I realized how lucky I was it was winter. The bridge was well guarded. But the frozen river was not. The ice hissed and eased a little, but did not give way. The next bad thing was a pass that I could not avoid. I could not make the broken mountainside in the dark. I had to use the pass. I walked very carefully toward it, and saw that there was a guard, and a tent with, I suspected, three other guards. A lantern was glowing in the tent. I crept within twenty feet of the guard before I blew his head off with three rounds from the carbine. Even before I had pulled the trigger on the carbine, I had pulled the pin to my one grenade, and pitched it in the tent before the noise of the third shot had ended. Two came out wounded and stupefied and I killed them quickly. I think the grenade had landed in the lap of the other. From the pass, I caught the glint of the ocean a few miles away. I did not know why only four men had been left at the pass, since the Chinese apparently sent out whole companies for the slightest task, but I was pleased it had been so. The next few miles of road were quiet and empty. It wasn't much of a road anyway, dirt, single lane, and whatever village it went to was not deemed of much importance by the Chinese. They knew they had chased our troops far south of it.

The village was so small I wouldn't have noticed it but for the dogs. They set up a terrible racket and I expected men to pour out of the houses ready to take on whatever intruder. But then I remembered this was war, and the poor people in the houses, if there were any left, were probably terrified that the dogs were signaling the approach of a brigade of looting and raping Chinese. Not a soul stirred. I, William Gasper, age 18, stalked through the village, a moonlight conqueror. The dogs howled as I walked to the tiny wharf, picked out a small but tidy fishing boat, one of three moored there, started the motor, and cast off. I was 500 yards offshore before I saw the first movements of people on the dock. The boat was about a 25-footer with a one-lung diesel, and would do about ten knots. I let it. Three or four miles offshore, I turned the bow southeast, and gave myself up to some well-deserved exhaustion. I didn't really sleep, but dozed a bit, keeping one eye on the stars, and another on the black wisp of the coastline, where I saw an occasional light. The sea was pretty quiet, and the adrenaline I had been living on for a long while gradually subsided, and I was almost smiling. Just about then, right in my ear, a voice said calmly, "That was quite a snowstorm, wasn't it, sailor?" I about shit. I turned with more control than I knew I possessed and looked at the woman beside me. She was wearing one of those white traditional garments of Korean women, with a gray cloak over her shoulders. Her hair was dark, but her features were Caucasian, not Korean. The English words had been pronounced carefully, but perfectly. It was hard to see her face clearly. It was as if swift movement or some astigmatism in my eyes made the final focus go askew. I didn't know what to say, or how.

"If you'll put the bow a few more points to port, you'll intercept a DE in a few miles. They might stop for you if they don't sink you first." I had not taken my eyes off her face, and there were moments when it seemed as though I were gazing directly at the moon, white in the sky, and then that would fade, and the woman emerge again for a moment. My hands moved the tiller, and the bow edged left against the horizon. "That's it," she said. "Hold it there."

The boat had an open cockpit, and resembled somewhat a Navy whaleboat. Nets were piled forward of the small engine compartment, there was a tiny decked-over shelter just aft of it. I could touch the shelter with my foot as I sat by the tiller. I was hunched against the thwarts, pulled down out of the wind, and resting my bones, so I guess she was sitting, too. But it is hard to remember. I was about as exhausted as I could get. At times I think of her standing beside me, nearly as tall as I was, and then again I remember the woman sitting beside me on the deck, her legs drawn up and covered by the cloak, her gaze steady at the bow. In one of those moments when I was caught by what seemed to be the moon filling her face, her voice broke through, saying, "I gave you a useful snowstorm. I'll give you another some day, perhaps for a different use." She paused, and her eyes hardened, though her smile was the same. "You call me Cerridwen, sailor. Don't bother to talk much about me, it won't do any good. You'll see me again, as well as when you die." At the instant her words were finished, a heavy beam of light hit the cockpit, and I was on my feet waving at a destroyer escort bearing down on me. When I looked again for her, she was gone. "As well as when you die." In all the confusion of the next few moments, yelling, waving, searchlights, boat maneuvers, and rescue, those words didn't leave me. AS WELL AS WHEN YOU DIE.

The Navy was decent to me. I got a few quick questions, some hot food, and a warm rack, where I slept about twenty hours. Then I got some more questions, and was told that the USS Humphrey had just begun its patrol, and would be at sea for another two weeks. I was TAD with them till they hit port, and assigned to their master-at-arms till then. The MA, a Chief Bosun with about thirty-seven years in, decided I could learn to make coffee and keep track of the duty rosters, and muster the twelve prisoners-at-large three times a day. (Being a prisoner-at-large generally meant you had come down with the clap, and were restricted to the ship for thirty days; or, it might mean you had fucked up slightly somewhere along the way, and were awaiting a Captain's Mast for some offense against the majesty and dignity of the armed forces.) It was just another way to harass the troops. Muster at 0600, 1200, and 2000. Always last in the chow line is what it meant.

I didn't say a word about Cerridwen to anyone. I've never been much of a talker anyway, and when you start gassing off about cloak-clad ladies who disappear in a puff of light and whose faces are sometimes the moon, you are headed toward a Section Eight forthwith.

The sea was new to me, though I had crossed the Pacific a few months before. But that hadn't been sea-duty, and I was really coming to like the mechanism of the ship, the coordination of men's lives with the throb of the engines, and the hull's subtle twisting in response to the waves. We ranged up and down the Korean coast, occasionally firing some rounds from our five-inchers to support the ground troops on the coast, but mostly we were like roving highway patrolmen, ready to intercept illegal traffic. The North Koreans had a few torpedo boats, and kept sending small groups of guerrillas down the coast in civilian hulls, and we tried to make life miserable for them. We shot at all we saw, and sank some, and made the others turn tail and run up on the beach. It wasn't a bad life.

For a few days we cruised far to the north, as though we were heading to Vladivostok, and that night the wind whipped out of Siberia with a polar chill. In general, though it was the dead of winter, the cold I had felt in the mountains was there in the mountains still, but not at sea. The waters warmed things. But that night the wind carried the cold so swiftly the waters had no chance to warm it, and it was like being on the ridges again, where the cold becomes a dreadful enemy, intent on wringing every calorie from your body, sucking every bit of warmth from you, and leaving you a husk, frozen, dead, as cold as the moon.

It was that night I came closest to saying something about Cerridwen, because the more I thought about her, the more she frightened me. But I didn't. Chief Russell had the imagination of a penguin, and the humor of a jackass, and I knew what he would do with such a sea story. I hadn't made any other friend, being a taciturn back-woodsman by nature. I was also a Jarhead and sailors who honor tradition have little to say to Jarheads.

Like the snowstorm on the ridge, which had enveloped the Chinese and permitted my escape, there came a time when Cerridwen spun another storm, this time in my mind, and I would forget completely about her for long periods. The memory would not disappear, but be obscured. As I thought back on my own behavior these past few days I realized I had not thought of Cerridwen at all when my Eye had told me I was followed. Yet who could it be but she? It is more than dangerous to face an adversary who can cloud one's mind. I had long understood this, as I had accepted the certainty that once, now or later, when she appeared to me, she would carry my own death in her hands.

〜〜〜 〜〜〜 〜〜〜

The Palug's ridge dropped steeply below me as I squatted at the lip of the highest series of cliffs, the last of the four steps. The rock was dark gray, a rather gritty granite, with both horizontal and vertical cracks. It offered the kind of climb that a halfway decent climber could solo easily enough, with only an occasional twinge of anxiety at certain moves. One system of cracks offered a straightforward descent, and I moved down it quickly, finding plenty of good jam holds, and enough horizontals that my legs could do most of the work. I thought the Palug cat probably expected me to wait for him at the top of his stairs, and I preferred not to be there, but somewhere else, when we met. The sense of exposure to height charged my body with a little adrenaline, like a clarifying hit of Colombian, and I played with the tactile wonder of holding my life with my fingers over the void.

I was in my mind a luckless wretch in high school, shy, twisted, ungainly, awkward, inept, and a loser. I could do nothing but read fast and shoot well. And then one year I discovered weightlifting and gymnastics, and turned the task of making my skinny body supple and strong. It worked. Within a few months, though still basically skinny, I was as strong as whang leather, and my tenacious grip was the object of considerable wonder. I had been doing a lot of chins to strengthen my arms and back, and had found that I could chin by hooking on to the bar with the middle finger of each hand. That led me to try the other fingers, and I was soon able to do a chin with any pair, and one middle finger alone. This not only comforted my battered ego, but was fine training for hard rock-climbing. I also won most of the finger-pulling contests I ever got into.

When I reached the bottom of the cliffs, I had about a quarter of a mile to the lip of the next step, down a steep slope. I moved fast, as I wanted to find just the right spot to watch the Palug cat make his ascent. I would meet him at the third step, and not the fourth. I had to decide whether to kill him from ambush and be done with it, or make his acquaintance, find out who he was, or who he claimed to be, and then decide what to do with him. If he were the Palug cat, I should kill him forthwith. If he were not, I probably shouldn't. He could be simply a wandering backpacker, as intent on the beauty of The Moon as I. Or he might be someone from the company, out checking on me again. If that were the case, an accident was better than a shooting. I was very much in favor of shooting him at a nice place on the climb where a solid fall would result, as I have always liked that kind of dramatic finality. But I know Cerridwen well enough that all this might be some vapor of imagination. It's always difficult, dealing with that creature. She might enjoy having me snuff an illusion, pump five rounds into a phantom, or into a vacationing Coptic scholar, or Buick dealer (though I thought it unlikely a Buick dealer would have such an avocation as walking The Moon).

How do you tell if it's the Palug cat you've got? Well, you can always look for narrow irises, or wait for the damn thing to leap over your head, turn in mid-air, and be ready with a knife by the time it lands. It's not something you inquire into carelessly. And it is why the notion of shooting him at first and best opportunity seemed the solution. All the old bushwhackers I knew had lived by following such clear logic, the old doctrine of waste and save.

I was sitting back from the rim a few feet, well hidden in a niche, looking down at the third step and the approaches to it. Down and to my right a big thumb of granite split off from the cliff and raised itself fifty or sixty feet in the air, in the same way that Lost Arrow splits and rises from the Yosemite rim, though on a tiny scale. The tip of the thumb was about ten feet in diameter, and stood out twenty or twenty-five feet from the top of the cliff, and perhaps fifteen feet lower. There was a reasonably easy route to the top of the thumb from the base, following a crack system. It might make a nice perch for a Palug cat to answer questions from. It might.

CHAPTER 3

I COULD SEE the Palug's ridge well enough from my niche, and I was protected from view both from below and from above. I shifted the pistol from my back pocket, and nestled it in the handwarmer pocket of my parka. It was a tidy and reassuring shape. I shouldn't have too long to wait. The afternoon sun burned bright on my forehead, and out of the wind I could feel a trace of warmth. It reminded me of many a sniper's perch I had inhabited for hours, though in those days my weapons had been more impressive—M-14, match grade, with an eight-power scope had been my favorite. For a while in Korea I had had a fine old Springfield which spoke with authority out to a thousand yards. With my .300 Weatherby, now resting back in the packing case at Sterns, I had connected with some regularity at 1500 yards on a still day all over Southeast Asia. It did love distance, that rifle! Well, I was good for a cantaloupe or a human head to about 75 yards with my SIG. Enough. One tiny piece of metal spinning into the control center was usually enough.

It is a simple matter to sit quietly watching, after one has mastered monotony. I have studied cell walls with the avidity of a scholar deep in an ancient text, and benefited as much thereby, as well. I am no longer in the cell, nor was I, long. I spent a few idle moments letting my glance rise from the ridge and float over the desert miles beyond. A distant view is the most soothing thing I know, and explains my predilection for deserts. Clear air, a stripped landscape and mountains are the reason Iceland remains my favorite country, though the rock there is abominable climbing, nasty rotten basalt that offers only frustration. But the views are the greatest on earth. It is as I imagine Mars to be, a pure, thin atmosphere that cherishes light as a diamond does, exploding in brilliance everywhere. My days alone in Iceland, wandering the center, were the happiest I have ever known, given some exhilarating flavor by the omnipresent light of an Arctic summer, and the winds that were like solid geometries. I believe I loved the place as well because I had no need to go armed. My Manchurian knife did camping tasks, but I had nothing around me that could explode, and was glad. I am enamored of weapons, truly, and enslaved to them by that, enslaved, too, because of my past, the course my life has taken. I have engaged in violence I did not anticipate until it has become habitual. I am not a peaceable man, much as I regret it. But in Iceland I was freed of the dominion of violence, for a little while. So I remember that, along with the views.

To the other world, one song goes with wandering, the one with the line, "Of home have I none," and most folks wisely refuse the inclination. Home is too precious to lose. But for some of us, home is so rudely taken, either swiftly, or cruelly, or by some default, that we have ever a reluctance for such attachment again. I thought of my own home at Sterns, a packing case for some large piece of mining machinery, tightened up a bit, insulated, roughly furnished, and all mine. It was ridiculous, but serviceable. My favorite home in recent years was a barn with a snug tack room where I had bunk and stove, bookcase and lantern, a table, and a tap of cold water from the tank outside. In the barn itself I parked my pickup, and from the rafters hung my Roman rings, which engaged my attention for three hours a day that year. Yes, an Iron Cross, and a fine planchet, front and back, though not that one-armed planchet of Gill's. I am too stringy yet, my arms too long. I had even space for a fifty-foot range, and practiced much with pistol and my old .22 target rifle. A good year in a barn! Never lonely, never discovered, and happier than a wanderer had a right to be.

I awoke in the gray before dawn, and ran for an hour, eight or nine miles, in a wide circuit shaped a little like a heart. It kept me fresh, and assured me of the nature of any stranger. Returned, muscles warmed and limbered, I would breakfast in the morning light, rest, then begin my work on the rings.

The simplest movements in gymnastics are

a music of dynamics and geometry. Timing, coordination, strength, and knowledge all play their part, and none may be missing. I was pleasantly remembering my repertoire, movement by movement, feeling the urges of old kinesthetic memory flicker in my arms and chest, when the Palug cat appeared on the ridge below. He hauled himself over the last step a quarter of a mile away, stood for a moment scanning the hill before him, shifted his pack, freshened his grip on his rifle, and began walking to the last step, where I perched, hidden on its edge. I let my eyes unaided follow him for a few moments, and then took a look through my monocular. Brown parka, dark green pants, a watch cap. He shifted the rifle, cradling the barrel in the crook of his right elbow, so he was indeed left-handed. I wondered if he had a pistol. I expected no trouble getting him to drop the rifle and climb obediently to his perch, but if he had a pistol, I would have to be less dramatic in my questioning than I would like.

He trudged up the hillside with a steady gait, good rhythm, good balance, good wind. As he drew nearer, the features of his face began to form themselves. It was a beautifully nondescript face, the bane of policemen and witnesses—a face one could never be sure of having seen before, even minutes earlier. Dreams create such faces, and our lady of the remainder.

The pack he carried was modest in size, which I approved of, and the rifle was nearly identical with my own—a left-handed bolt action. As he worked his way up the steep hillside in short switchbacks, I noted with some satisfaction how like me he was, though blondish. Long arms and legs, and a watchful habit. No beard, hair cut short, or at least held in by the watch cap. His stride was much the same as my own. It was a little like watching a movie of myself working up a hillside, and I began to suspect the worst of Cerridwen. If my brother Paul had not been long dead, a suicide at thirty, the figure might well be he, trudging up to a dig somewhere in Turkey, mumbling some fragment of Archilochos.

I watched him move closer with fascination, and each new signal of some old intimacy, personal or fraternal, increased both doubt and certainty. The more he appeared to be some version of me or my brother, the more I doubted the coolness with which I expected to perforate his brain pan, the more, that is, I hesitated in my resolve. And yet, the more he emerged as doppelgänger or clone, the more I knew him the work of Cerridwen, and as much a fiend from hell, if there were fiends, or hell. Yet, why would she pull such a juvenile trick? All she could hope for by it was some tiny moment of indecision. Or maybe not. I felt a deep apprehension then, and the certainty I had about Cerridwen's basic malevolence shifted. I had known for long, or believed for long, that from her point of view, she was not malevolent—had she been, she simply would have squeezed me out of the world like a pimple. No, from her point of view she was just playing. But she didn't really understand human fragility—her physical powers were too great, and her time perspective too long. Playing with her was like trying to surf through a hurricane. This is what I had thought, and with good reasons. But as I watched the Palug cat clamber over some low rocks, choosing the same path I would have, I wondered. I could see now through the monocular a pleasantly bland smile on his face, the same smile that came so easily to my own, and I knew I didn't know what I was going to do.

Nor, I thought, with a sudden jerk of my head and a rush of hate for the Hag, should I let my mind be linted and fuzzed by reverie and silly memory. If Cerridwen was going to kill me this time, she must do it herself. The Palug had reached the base of the cliffs, and paused a moment as he studied them. I got two very rapid hollow points into his skull before he began to topple, and one more in the first few seconds after he fell to the ground. As I watched his still figure, I pushed the magazine release, and quickly reloaded. He did not move, and I did not think he ever would.

I waited a few minutes, my mind in a tense hush, my chest tight with adrenaline. After the crash of the 9mm the quiet of the mountain seemed oppressive, as though the whole world were holding its breath. My own breathing, and the steady, heavy banging of my heart in my neck was all I could feel. "What a work is man," I muttered to myself as I straightened up from my sniper's post, and began to climb down the cliff.

The Palug's face oozed blood, the back of his skull was shattered and open. After a careful scrutiny of his features, which did not in the least resemble my own or my brother's, I pulled the watch cap down like a death mask, or miniature shroud, and began to examine his effects. The rifle was undamaged, though I should fire it later to check the zero. It was a Remington BDL in .270, quite new, and left-handed. A tight, lovely little rifle. There was no wallet, no identification, but a money clip made with a Double Eagle in his front pocket had $6500 in it, including five one thousand dollar bills. No watch. His boots were Super Cervinos, Italian. They are very heavy, tough boots, and the only thing out of keeping for a cat. They looked new, or nearly so, and I doubted they were broken in yet. Boots like that take a year or two of hard walking in to finally feel decent. I wondered if the Palug's feet had been sore.

His pack was a Karrimor Jaguar, again new, a British make not seen in this country often. I was quite willing to bet that Cerridwen had been shopping some place like Alpine Sports on Holborn Street. Probably at their last Christmas sale. The contents were normal—a Svea stove and cook set, a bottle of gas, freeze-dried food, a very nice sleeping bag, better than my own, forty rounds of .270, extra socks, an Icelandic pullover, a small first aid kit with moleskin (his feet had been sore) and some Dexedrines. In the zippered map pocket were two topo maps of The Moon, folded around a British passport. The photo in the passport did not look particularly like the cat, but that was not surprising. The name was Brewster Shallot, born in Swansea, 1938. The pages were heavily stamped, and indicated considerable European travel, especially in Scandinavia, with two or three trips to India, Thailand, Hong Kong, and Japan.

I unlaced the Cervinos and pulled them off his feet. Then I dragged him over to a crevice at the base of the cliff and stuffed him in. I spent about half an hour covering his body with heavy rocks. It wasn't likely he would ever be found.

The boots were a half size too big, but I added a pair of his fine woolen socks and knew I could leave his tracks for the rest of the day. My own boots are not really boots, but rock climber's EB's—like heavy tennis shoes with a smooth sole of rather soft rubber. I find they move very quietly. I repacked the Karrimor, picked up his rifle, slung it on my shoulder, and climbed up on the cliff. When I glanced back at the dried blood on the rocks where the cat had fallen, I said nothing to myself and did not let my eyes waver.

I was over the last of the cliffs and heading toward the junction of the Palug's ridge with mine before I thought of anything at all. I had kept my attention on the ground and footing, moving the boots and their unaccustomed weight with special care. My mind had slipped into the distance runner's white noise, though the dim sensation of wearing buckets on my feet slipped through. As I stood at the junction and looked out onto the desert beyond The Moon, the afternoon sun late and gold in the sky, I very carefully placed the Palug cat, in this guise, anyway, in a deep black canyon of memory. I would not forget his face, with the small bruised bullet holes, nor the black watch cap I pulled over it. But I would see it again only at my will, at my particular call. He would not pollute my dreams. It is a matter of discipline, not coldness, as any surgeon can tell you.

In a few minutes I was back at the outcrop where I had left my pack. No more errands were left for the day, and so I settled back, made a pillow of the Karrimor, took off the Palug's buckets, and let my eyes rest on the horizon as I half-dozed. I loved to lie that way, poised above sleep, but full of sleep's tranquillity; alert, yet resting. I could feel my limbs lighten as the muscles relaxed down to the bone. I lay there about an hour, judging from the movement of the sun, and then began to feel an urge for tea. The Palug's stove worked quite well, and in a few minutes I had water to the boil. After tea I checked the zero of the rifle.

The cartridges were loaded with the fast 130-grain bullet, with a flat trajectory which permitted a nice combination: zero at 250 yards, with the bullet two inches high at 100, and four inches low at 300. I picked out a lichen-covered rock about 250 yards away on the west slope of the ridge, well lighted now from the side, and rested the fore-end on the pack. Two shots told me to move the sight two clicks left. The third round was in, and for insurance, the fourth. The thunder of the first report shocked me, and I wished I had brought my ear plugs. For all the shooting I've done, I don't like loud noises. And somehow, through all the wars, my hearing has remained acute. I guess it was because I was never around artillery that much, and had plugged my ears when I could.

If there were anyone else on The Moon this day, within a mile or two, the shots revealed a presence. If it were my lady Cerridwen, well, she might be wondering what mouse her Palug had taken with his thunderstick. Maybe she knew, or thought she knew. Whatever, that was for later. Now I reloaded, and set the rifle aside as I considered what to do.

I had belled the cat, or some poor limey tourist, but I had the Hag on my trail, if my suspicions were correct. The tentacles of feeling I called my Eye still insisted someone, a woman, followed. Well, if I am to be followed, let me be leader, and tonight sleep on the very peak of The Moon. I liked that notion, and set to work with my gear. I would take the Palug's rifle and ammunition, the money clip, passport, and maps. I also coveted his new sleeping bag, so I stuffed that into my pack. This left room for the buckets and my old bag in his Karrimor, and I hung the shapely pack on a sliver of rock at the back of the outcrop, well out of the weather. It could hang there for years and probably be well preserved, and perhaps the next wanderer along would have need of those buckets.

I slipped my pack on, took a long look down my ridge, and then turned toward the peak of The Moon, another five miles away, and about

1500 feet higher. The Moon rode 14,561 feet above sea level, one of the lost Fourteeners. No one knew if it had ever been climbed, and no one cared. I had climbed it many times, and I did not care. I often slept on top because it was as close as I could get to the sky hereabouts, and I often yearn for something in the sky. The top was noisy with wind some nights, and often more cold than pleasant, but the stars were incontestable, knowing that the land fell away from me on all sides, and I was being thrust up into the heavens like a dust mote balanced on the tip of a meaninglessly huge finger.

I cradled the rifle in my right arm and walked slowly, savoring the light and the wind. The sky was free of clouds now, though a delicate hint of moisture remained in the air, and the going along the ridge was smooth. I would rather walk a ridge than anything. I like being high, and looking at the land falling away on both sides, as though I were tightrope walking. I remembered that even when I had been hunted, I traveled by ridges rather than valleys.

CHAPTER 4

THE GREYHOUND at my uncle's ranch had taught me the laws and spirit of killing. It was a simple, good-natured dog, treated offhandedly, as were most of the ranch dogs. Some helped herd sheep, in an ignorant but effective way, others were alarms and guards at the corrals and ranch house, and two or three, including the greyhound, spent their time traveling with us as we did our work. We rode the forty square miles of the ranch in look of broken fence or ailing windmills, sheep infected with screw worm, wandered cattle, or any other trouble that a merciless nature can inflict on a poor rancher. Our days were full. It was a year of drought, at the pit of the seven-year cycle common to southern New Mexico, and creatures had grown perverse as they had grown thirsty and the grass they ate snapped off in their mouths like tiny blades of chalk.

We rode thirty or so miles a day, enough to lather a horse without pushing it harder than a trot, and enough to weary my backside. In the last hour of riding, homebound on a flat cut by a dusty creek bed, the greyhound cruised in wide circles to flush a rabbit. He always did, and chase with a true winner and loser would ensue. A big jack rabbit can outrun a horse for most useful distances, and come close to outrunning a greyhound. But generally not quite. The jack rabbit knew he had lost the race when something snapped his backbone and began to tear him apart. The greyhound ate his catches, and even shared them with the slower dogs. Something fast and hungry ate something not so fast.

It was not enough simply to be fastest. It was necessary to be motivated to use that speed. Hunger motivates, so does fear. But most of all, intelligence. That is why our species is the greatest hunter and predator the earth has seen. Waste and save, snuff and breathe. If it moves and can be killed, it is probably good to eat. It is a residuum from the earliest moments of man, even before he became man. Life feeds on life, and does so by killing. We manage our affairs well enough that such extreme choices are rare. But they are not unknown. And at those moments, the men whose genes and conditioning remember most of the old ways come into their own again. Some are warriors, and move openly, loudly, meeting their foes to the accompaniment of drumbeats and TV coverage. Others are assassins, and take their prey by stealth. Each performs a useful task for the group which employs him, or owns his loyalty.

I am an assassin, as much by nature as by trade. There are fewer of us than warriors, I suspect, for it is easier to listen to drumbeats and find the feet moving in cadence than to sit alone in the dark, waiting. But this is my natural prejudice, and I won't pursue it. I would merely assert that an assassin may be as fully heroic, virtuous, patriotic, and glory-driven as any warrior. There are even some of us who are family men, though we practice objectivity. It must be clear that no assassin can be a romantic. Warriors are romantics. Assassins, if they are not simply cold, and many are, learn to act with the great and pious deliberation of classicists. Do not confuse us with generals, for whom the encounters of war can be no more than a sophisticated game. We assassins meet our foes with no intermediaries, as fully, perhaps more fully, than does the warrior. We work most often alone, sometimes in small teams, and it is only when we fail that our names become known. But it is finally we who decide the fatal instant. Our hands and fingers do the work.

I have often speculated why we assassins are considered more immoral than other killers for the state. It has something to do with a romantic vision of fair play, a distaste for treachery, and some "playing fields of Eton" illusion about sportsmanship and war. I have little patience with such casuistical arguments. Efficiency, accuracy, choice: these are the qualities one wants in a weapon. As a lancet takes a boil. And this is not a moral argument, though one might try to make it so; I will have no bother with morality or other phantoms. It is will and ability against will and ability. No more. Sometimes I think it was Cerridwen who taught me this, in whatever ways are her ways, over the years. One takes the attitude of a god, and let hubris be damned. Yet always act within your limits, knowing them precisely. Aim to be certain. Know your own weaknesses better than you know your enemy's—for the one is possible, and the other not.

This is becoming like lessons for the young assassin, as indeed it is. Behold the hunter and his prey. I have never hunted for sport. Only to eat. Warfare is a feast. Cold words, and were the heart's dread allowed to cloud the mind, who knows what chaos would come? The Hag can cloud my mind some way; I know that. I don't know why she has chosen me for her attention, or if it has to do with my trade, and she is some reflection of killing. There are times when I think of fucking her, and hold myself above her, hard and long, the glans of my penis guided back and forth between her labia, and her vagina like some stellar vacuum, ice cold, with the pull of a million suns. If I thrust in, and I do, my penis is sucked into a terrible maelstrom, and my body is stripped away from my brain, my mind.

Even now in the telling of it, I am distracted, and lost from my argument. I want her, I want that shredding, that spin into whatever galaxy her cunt inhabits. It is not this one, I am sure. It would be something, would it not, if the only door to hyperspace in this world were through some mythic doxy's twat? I don't even know if goddesses, or whatever she is, have cunts. She could well be a seamless simulacrum, with skin like panty hose. Distracted. I was talking of killing, then of the Hag, and fucking her, and off I went. Fancies and fantasies. But the last time she tried it I potted her cat with my lovely pistol. If she laughs it off, as I think she will, she still won't like it. Distract me, and I become very dangerous.

Values are a personal matter, whether of art, or love, or killing. These are matters of taste and convention, nothing more. As far as possible I have tried to act with reason and calmness in these things. I know what I like and I know what I want. I am even willing to sacrifice for others. If I want. I seldom want to, and that is one reason I have lived these years in such country as The Moon provides—wide and empty. A short, ugly service in the world of men provided the means, and I would not care to return. But I do not tolerate annoyance, whether by the Hag or some acronymic brotherhood.

The assassins history takes most note of are amateurs, ill-trained, suicidal, driven by passion or insanity, or the perversions of politics. Of short stature often, with absent fathers and domineering mothers. And these amateurs change history, for their targets are usually presidents or kings, despots, or men eager to become such. A professional assassin will ordinarily have nothing to do with an attempt on such public figures. They are too well guarded; and even if the assassin makes his kill, he is often captured or killed. Only in the most extreme circumstances would a professional take on such a task. No, the targets of the true assassin are personages of the second or third level of power—a district police officer, a judge, an industrialist, a banker, a diplomat below the rank of ambassador. The elimination of these figures can be accomplished with no more than a modest police investigation or press campaign, and their removal can shift the local processes just enough to make the risk and the price acceptable. You would be surprised how many assassinations, especially in business, are brought about not by competitors from another company, but by forces within the victims' own offices. The mark of the professional assassin is no mark, of course, a natural death, an accident. It is only by an actuarial study that such deaths are noticed, and that does not happen often. Then all the actuaries do is skew the curve a little and note a new, if ill-defined, risk for certain types of executives.

My own special area of expertise was the elimination of middle rank military and investigative officers. I am not interested in the chicanery of politics or industry, but warfare and suchlike came to me early, and I learned much from warriors, even to be one when needed.

I also rather like the military's ability to draw a veil over its activities, and, as well, to make the most squalid back alley snuff something of virtuous moment. I murder for the state, and that is supposed to give my acts legitimacy, if not nobility. It is a lie, of course, and I know my acts are not different because of motive. To kill willfully is to kill willfully, whether it is for money, for revenge, for patriotism, for idealism, or for simple anger. The difference, perhaps, is that one's society does not punish for killing at its direction, and one's conscience is supposed to be clear. It pays, as it does for any service it needs. We do not judge the act, or even the man, when we hang one as a scoundrel, and bemedal the other as a hero. We judge only the effect on society. And as for conscience, it is the clustering pulsations of conditioned neurons, and nothing more. Conscience is a social lubricant; it reflects our awareness of the rules which make the game playable. But conscience should never bind intelligence. Guide, but not bind.

God, I weary of lectures! They spin out of me constantly when I am on the move, as a spider drools web. If words could be tracked like footprints, my silent passages would be an electric crimson trail. It is because I spend so much time alone, I tell myself, grunting at the very words. I can sit and hardly muse, and on a long run I can pass over into the float. But walking, trudging, my mind insists on words. Doubtless I serve my fellow man better as an assassin than I would as pedagogue, for in a classroom I would paralyze thirty minds an hour, pacing in front of the desk, covering the decline of the ablative in the reign of Justinian.

I must have been more nervous than I realized, for several times the chatter in my mind distracted my attention enough that I stumbled, catching the edge of my foot on a rock. The ridge was no steeper, but it was rougher, with innumerable small cuts twenty or so feet deep, and forty or fifty across, the rocks horse-sized. From behind me an alpenglow began to tint the rocks as the sun edged closer to the horizon. When I came to the next little cleft, I paused and slipped off my pack. It was time for a breather, and a sip of brandy. I leaned the rifle against the pack, and pulled the brandy from my parka. I could see far back down the ridge, and at the point where it met the horizon, the dark slope of the Palug's ridge running off and down to the left. I could see the last two steps of cliffs there, the farthest now the place where the Palug lay, the last of his body heat dissipating, sucked into the cold rocks which weighted him as a building weighs on its foundations. So new to it, he was already a part of The Moon. Of course, whether the Palug was really firmly attached to the flesh, I knew not. Moon-face might have already clothed him with a dog's carcass, or stuffed him into a blackbird. Skinwalkers, the Navahos call such attendants, and one doesn't speak lightly of them. Such things may take over the body of any creature killed for the purpose, or perhaps any dead thing come across. I don't know. Anomalies are real enough. Who can believe what is written of black holes?

I took another sip of brandy and held it in my mouth, rinsing it back and forth over my teeth, under and around my tongue until I felt afire, and then I swallowed. Damnfuck the Hag! She was interfering with my walk. I picked up the rifle and sighted through the scope down the ridge. Nothing moved that I could see. If I slept deeply enough tonight, perhaps my Eye would travel and bring me something better than a dream tomorrow. But I was not at all sure of sleeping well, given the puzzle apparently set me.

While the brandy still warmed my throat, I took up the pack and rifle and clambered down the side of the cleft in the ridge. In the shadow I could feel the bite of colder air. Dusk was coming, and the night would be below freezing here. A bank of hard-pressed snow, nearly ice, lay in the shadow, and I had to kick half a dozen steps to make my way to the bottom. There was a trickle of run-off there, and I knelt and chased the brandy with some handfuls of water. After that, I moved fast, making a mile over the rough, broken ridge in half an hour. The terrain smoothed then, and the ridge lay unbroken except for one knife cut a hundred yards or so before the top. The point and center of The Moon, its apex, was less than a mile away. I was at a little over 14,000 feet now, and I could feel a slight shortness of breath when I pushed hard up a slope. I acclimatize rapidly, and this was no great height, but I needed to remember that I might be three or four per cent off my best, if I were called to do my best. I believe in such little reminders. It's like with the Army .45—the most sensible way to carry the piece is with a round in the chamber, the hammer cocked, and the safety on. It's quite safe, and it is quick to put into action. But many people feel uneasy with the hammer back. The pistol looks as if it might go off so easily, the hammer back, aching to let to. But this is the illusion, what the reminder must correct. Perception and reality must be as congruent as one can make them.

Illusion, legerdemain. The ridge now was a ledge, as easy to walk as the trail between Saks and Bloomingdale's. The view was good, and I felt a little petty that I did not pause to enjoy it more fully, but I was in no mood for poems on the moon breaking in two over Kweilin, or a crane eating perch from a rice field. Esthetics, despite many fair tales to the contrary, has absolutely nothing to do with survival. It may be the key to my presence here at all, but not my circumstance now. I pushed hard, pushed my shadow up the ridge in front of me, the golden light reddening, and a dusk growing in the east. The brandy had stimulated my appetite, and I was ready for a little supper. Too bad I had been so busy I had not paused to lure a grouse within pot range. I had the sudden image of me tearing into a raw grouse, the feathers ripped from the breast before a bite, with a wild look in my eye. It was an image I thought Gail Henry had of me often, especially after I had told her a good way to prepare locusts or grubs.

The knife cut in the ridge was perhaps a hundred feet deep, a little tougher than a scramble going down with a rifle, but no worse going up. More patches of hard snow hid in the shadows, and the very bottom was decidedly gloomy. I rested a moment at the bottom of the cleft, and for a few seconds I was caught up in images from the Inferno, or the eleventh book of the Odyssey where the mouth to the world of the dead opened soundlessly, and the spirits of great warriors twittered in the depths like bats, or the rustle of footsteps through dry leaves. It was a somber place, cut from the sun's rays by dark gray granite, and pulled even deeper into darkness by its own angles and curves.

Such places, when they are accessible to the multitudes, generate a considerable philosophical error, being perfect spots for the afflatus of the mysterium tremendum to afflict the mind of man. A few hours spent in the shadows, listening to the wind moan above your head, and demons would be an easy enough conceit. And wouldn't my prune-nippled Hag slaver to find me camped in such a spot? I had no wish to give her any better odds than I had her Cat. Not, I admitted to myself, that I had much to do with setting the odds in this world. I craned my neck, studied the route out, slung the rifle to free both hands, and started up.

I was not more than twenty minutes making the ascent. It was mainly a matter of picking footholds and maintaining balance. I was slow enough that the elegance of my movements nearly disappeared, but I felt satisfied with the chain of solutions I knotted as I faced each new problem moving up. At the top, I glanced back down into the dark pit, and shook the shadows from me. On the ridge, the last of the ridge, the gold-red glow of the sunset led my way to the summit. There was no cairn there, no climbers' log. The absolute top was a granite boulder about six feet high and twelve across, and I had made it my bed before. I hoisted the pack up, slid the rifle beside it, and clambered up. In every direction, The Moon fell away from me like the folds of a vast robe. From the point I looked out with the eyes of The Moon herself, was herself.

The air was still, so I lit the stove in the open and boiled water for my tea and gruel. While I let the tea steep in my canteen cup, I mixed a handful of powdered milk, confectioner's sugar, and ground Brazil nuts with the soy. It made a paste fit for a paperhanger, but it had the calories I needed. Perhaps tomorrow I would find the grouse. The boulder was throne and dining table all in one, and soon enough would become a bed. Night was coming, and I finished sipping the tea with my eyes on the land below the horizon, where a pinprick of light would signal a traveler. There was none. The night deepened as though the mountain top were sinking into the sea.

I pulled the Ensolite pad and Cat's sleeping bag from the pack, unrolled and fluffed it, pulled off my shoes and trousers, and climbed in, resting my back against the pack. It was as much comfort as I had felt all day. I kept the pistol nestled loosely in my hand, and the rifle easy by my side. As I stretched my legs in the bag, my toes discovered a small package at the bottom. I fished it out. About two and a half inches by six, and perhaps an inch thick, wrapped in clear plastic, heavy at one end. It was however many hundred dollar bills there are to the inch and a roll of sixteen Kreugerands. If the Hag had paid her Cat before he finished his labors, all the better. I might go to Las Vegas and buy a whore with her money, just for spite. But first I must finish my dalliance with The Moon, and see a few more nights pass by. I pushed the money back to the bottom of the bag, and turned my attention to sleep.

CHAPTER 5

THE DREAM always begins in exile and fear, in paranoia. I am usually walking down a street near a waterfront, or a canal. It is at once Saigon and Hamburg. My destination is a darkened warehouse some blocks away. I know the route, though I have never been there before, and I am pursued. The streets are wet, and there is an icy, knife blade flicker to the reflections of the streetlamps. I seem to be young, in my twenties, or even younger, eighteen perhaps. My thoughts, when they are not focused on my worry about pursuit, are of my home, lost now, and my dead parents. The loneliness is terrible, and depressing. I get no nearer the warehouse. It is there, nearby, but out of sight. I begin to notice small shops, groceries, taverns, galleries. I pass a cinema but I cannot read the marquee. People drift by, or step aside as I pass. They are nebulous, and I cannot get a clear focus on a face. They pay little attention to me, but are aware of my presence. I begin to worry that my pursuers are among them, or I begin to worry that I will be held up and robbed. There are figures at the edge of the darkness that talk to each other, and glance my way. I pick up my pace, and move my hands to my pockets, where my fingers trace lightly on my legs, searching for the comforting outline of my pistol or knife. My pockets are empty. My hand moves to my waistband and slips along it. No pistol. I try to make the surface of my skin reveal where I have hidden my weapon. It is not in a shoulder holster, not in an ankle holster. I cannot feel it anywhere on my body, and I frantically try to remember what I have done with it. All the time my fear is growing, and I believe that several figures are on my trail. At the next cross-street, I turn right suddenly, and break into a run, determined to lose those in pursuit. The block is tree-lined, and I measure my speed by the rapidity with which the trees flicker past, as though I were on a train or in a car, watching telephone poles slip by. I run a long while, until it becomes ridiculous and silly, and I threaten to awaken myself from the dream. But something holds me in the dream, and I feel a great urgency to find the warehouse, to make a connection there with something important. The urge to break out of the dream serves as a transition, and I usually find myself on a street with more shops, more people. There is a gaiety and bustle to the crowd, and the threat I felt eases. I pause and look into a shop window. It is a pawnshop, and the window is full of pistols, Italian switchblades, cameras, musical instruments, binoculars, and trays of diamond rings. A young girl joins me at the window, and stands silently, absorbed in the display.

"I've always wanted one of those knives with the button," she said, still looking into the window. Then she turned to me and smiled. "Which one do you like?"

"I like the five-inch blade," I replied, trying and failing to place the girl in my memory.

"Let's go buy one," she said, putting her hand on my elbow as if I were her escort. "It won't take long at all. You can help me pick one out." Her smile was nice, and I felt no fear.

"Okay," I said, moving toward the door. "Maybe I'll buy one myself."

The door to the pawnshop had a heavy wire grille and three locks. It was silent when we stepped inside. I looked around at the counters, and found the one with a row of switchblades lying on a dark brown velvet cloth.

"Here they are," and I looked down at her face again. The light in the store showed me a pretty, dark-eyed girl, dark hair, a gray wool coat, a black scarf, maybe twenty years old, as tall as my shoulder. As we approached the counter, the proprietor emerged from the jewelry cage at the rear of the store and walked towards us.

"Can I help you folks?"

"We'd like to buy a knife," the girl said, "one of those with a button, and a five-inch blade." She pointed along the row of knives. "Like that one there," she gestured at a switchblade with white ivory handles. The man looked at her carefully, and then at me, making a quick assessment of us.

"That's real ivory, you know." He slid the back of the case open, reached in and lifted out the knife. He peered at the gummed price tag stuck to it. "It's eighty-five dollars. Real ivory." The girl had extended her hand, and he placed the knife there with a tiny flourish. She looked at it carefully, turning it about in her hand, weighing it. Then she carefully moved her fingertips back from the blade edge, and pushed the button with her thumb. She smiled as the blade flicked into place. She tested the lock and the fit of the blade to the handle. Then she very carefully touched the point and the honed edge.

"It's not as sharp as I thought it would be."

"Well, miss, it's more designed for sticking than for cutting," the proprietor said, his voice relaxed and low. "But you could put a decent edge on it if you wanted. It's very good steel."

"I'll take it," the girl said, opening her purse and taking out her wallet. She gave the man five twenties. He took the money, then paused and looked questioningly at me, as though he were either waiting for my approval, or to see if I wanted something myself. The girl turned, too, and for a moment they both looked at me, and then they began to wring their hands, their heads bobbing, mock agony on their faces. They began to chant, "What do you want? What do you want?" in singsong voices, their heads bobbing faster and faster.

I think for a moment I had been lulled by the

seeming normalcy of the dream, and had begun to accept its reality. But now the two frenzied puppets in front of me showed that reality to be spurious; all the earlier anxieties about being followed and failing to reach the warehouse, whatever its contents, were the simplest kind of dream transformation of the day's worries. In the middle of their ranting babble I woke myself, disgusted with my mind. Such simple tripe, such boredom. The quality of dreams could not possibly be related to the quality of the waking mind's thinking. Or at least I hoped not.

The night blazed at me with a few thousand more stars than lowlanders enjoy. The field of the sky seemed unusually deep, as though the stars beyond the stars stood out in a way I knew the human eye could not discern. There is no depth to the night sky, our eyes are too close together. And so our own eyes' witness can be bent by our desires.

With my eyes locked on the stars overhead, I thought about the dream, and what I did want. These last ten years of solitude and deliberate exile had eased the lock the previous twenty had been exerting on my mind. In 1969, a rage of tension and disillusionment at my own incapacity to maintain the slightest saving illusion seemed to be driving me to suicide. There comes a point, even to such a cynic and nihilist as I, when treachery seems so complete, so inescapable, that life becomes monstrous and repulsive. The only value I had ever found lay in the excitement of survival; and even that was easy to reduce to an addiction to adrenaline. I had believed once that I would be loath to kill the innocent, and thought to cloak my acts in the robes of justice. One of the Danites I was, one of the Avenging Angels. I found that is a paltry illusion, and cannot last a week in the field. A sniper's targets are always taken innocent and unaware, moral babies at the moment you explode their brains. I have killed one hundred and twenty-seven men and women, and not more than a dozen were doing anything at the moment of their death which might have warranted their death. I saved no prisoner from the flashing ax of the executioner an instant before it severed his head; I killed no torturer as he gloated over a screaming victim. The torturer I killed, one of them, was raising a spoon of chicken soup to his mouth when I filled it instead with an ounce of buckshot traveling at a thousand feet per second. The buckshot barely paused as it blew through his jaw and neck.

And even had I saved a thousand maidens from a fate worse than death, what virtue would I have garnered in a universe devoid of virtue? There was nothing out there for any of us. There was the body's delight in itself as long as that lasted, and there was death. Nothing else. Nothing was forbidden, nothing bidden. It simply was, and went on. Even the terror such a universe creates is a kind of fiction, a passing illusion. If it does not seem so to you, I suggest you have not served enough time in extremis yet, that fate has spared you the necessity for honest vision and clear conclusions. If you wish to keep such illusions, do not ask deeply of any who have spent a long time on the killing grounds of the world. For even the fools who say they act for an abstraction know in their dreams they lie. Duty, Justice, God, Country, Honor are but vanities.

I turned in the sleeping bag and shielded my eyes from the stars with one arm. It seemed there was no turning off the sermons that ran through my addled brain. If I wanted anything, it was to be rid of preachment, to silence the querulous asshole who mourned morality's extinction by reality. I knew who I was—an executioner, just like Charlie Sanson, who snuffed Louis XVI, or his son Henri, who did the honors for Marie Antoinette. I was not Kierkegaard, and if I have subtleties, I have trained them to be silent. Twenty years a master of the killing ground taught me that kind of silence, for a qualm that stays your hand for a millisecond may be your own death, and is a shameful professional error.

So what did I want? *Was will der Mensch?* I thought of becoming a rapist. I was already a mass murderer, but a piker compared with most bomber pilots, or any machine gunner who had seen more than a month of heavy action. And certainly I could not hope to compete with politicians with my paltry body count. Perhaps as a rapist I might leave some mark. But I had tried it and found it wanting. There is a small excitement to rape, but nothing of the languorous pleasure sex otherwise brings. I am not of that temperament, generally. One cannot rob who has such contempt for money, nor can one betray who is not first given to loyalty. The only reason I did not work for the KGB, or some other force for another truth, is that I was never asked. Killers, even with such skills as I possess, are not uncommon. We make ourselves known early in life, and the organ of our society that would make use of our talents is not long in discovering them. It so happens that the pulse of my life at eighteen beat with the particular needs of the Marines as I happened to be there, and so the river flowed, and I with it.

But this is not to say I might not have been plucked from the river and set on the bank claimed by another power, and worked as skillfully for it. Even as a child, I knew I was not above history.

So: I wanted to buy a knife, did I? What did that mean? Was my cock hungry for cunt? Did I want to push my button and have it spring hard and alive, and then to stab a woman between the legs? This was sophomoric Freudianism, but it could be saying something true about me. Who was the girl? Certainly not the Hag. But perhaps she was. I could not tell. I rolled to my other side, and opened my eyes again to the night. I fixed my eyes on Polaris and tried to gauge the spinning of the earth. I wanted no more images.

I awoke again at about 3:00 a.m. with a hand on my shoulder. "Wake up, sailor, The Moon would talk with you." I jerked awake in a panic, but the hand on my shoulder held me firm long enough for my eyes to take in a white face above mine, long hair brushing my face, and wide, cold eyes on mine. "Wake up, sailor, and tell me about my cat."

Her voice was calm, and her hand eased its grip as I struggled to sit up, and my hand searched for and found the pistol wedged under my leg. "Sit up, sailor, and talk to me." She released her grip on my shoulder and squatted before me on the boulder. Her hair was white and long to her waist. She was naked, her body that of a woman of thirty. Her breasts sagged with the curve of maturity, and the hair between her legs shone white in the moonlight, whiter than her pale skin. If she was beautiful she was also strange. My chest was tight with surprise and fear, and it was a moment before I could begin to move. If she were human and had wanted me dead, I would have been. That I wasn't intrigued me, as she had always intrigued me, in spite of the fear.

"Your cat was hunting me, Cerridwen," I said. "I don't like to be hunted any more."

Her mouth curled in a smile and she spit on the boulder. "It was a stupid cat this time," she said, her voice amiable. Her elbows rested on her knees as she waited for me to speak.

"I didn't have any trouble with it," I said finally. "I think its feet hurt in those boots."

She laughed out loud at that. "Yes," she nodded. "Yes, its feet hurt. It didn't know how to hunt or make trouble." Her right hand moved casually, and she began to scratch her butt. It was a gesture of delay, a gesture that signaled a search for a word in a foreign language. I had sat with Montagnard tribesmen and done the same thing, searching for some locution in Meo. "May I sit on your bed?" she finally asked, her hand pointing carefully at the foot of the bedroll.

I was astonished. She had never asked my permission for anything before. "Of course," I answered. "It's yours anyway." She slipped onto the down bag without, it seemed, making a motion, stretched out her legs and leaned back on her hands. The moonlight shone along her body, and it was obvious that she was aware of its effect on me.

"Yes," she said, "the cat could not hunt. But I can hunt." She spoke the words flatly, without malevolence. She leaned forward suddenly and placed the palm of her hand on my cheek. "Others can hunt, too," she went on, her eyes locking with mine. Her hand slid down to my chest. "And now, sailor, shall we? This is a good place."

With the same invisible effort she had displayed in moving onto the bedroll, she moved into it, giggling, her hands fast as snakes on my back. She slipped the pistol from my grip as though she were pulling off a glove, writhing sweetly against me. Her hand had cupped my penis and testicles, and she began to play with them as she pressed herself against me.

So what are the metaphysics of deception? There is nothing beyond physics, no hidden volume, no next study. Our knowledge stops with physics, which is sufficiently fanciful anyway. I don't know what Cerridwen is, or was. I was alone on a boulder at a mountain's tip, deep in the night, stars as pure as illusion overhead, my penis stiff and hard, and a hankering for woman-flesh in my mind. But totally alone, awake and alone.

It is not that dreams are more or less vivid than reality, but that they lose contact with the base. Dreams from one night to another rise from different bases, different worlds. The world we wake to each morning is the same, or most nearly so. So waking life denotes the real. I turned in my bag and wondered on these betrayals by the night, these returning clarities which would defy the day. For nearly thirty years I had lived in a world in which I went to sleep at night and often entered dream worlds of brief duration, and palpable unimportance. But also during those thirty years had come several episodes, always focusing on a figure I knew as Cerridwen, which were not dreams, and yet which defied the accepted rules of daylight's operation. Perhaps I was mad. Killers were often mad. Madness could well be the situation in which dreams seemed to arise from daylight's reality, as Cerridwen arose in my days or nights. I felt as perplexed as old Chuang Tzu, who dreamt so vividly of being a butterfly that when he awoke, he could not decide if he had simply dreamt of being a butterfly, or was a butterfly dreaming he was Chuang Tzu. It is a dilemma not easy to resolve.

For example, if in the earlier dream there had been a press of crowds outside the pawnshop, crowds lining the road, and a heavy car driving by, top down, a smiling man and woman waving to the crowds, and a quick succession of shots, then it could have been a dream as I understand them, dredging shards of memory from the deeps, distorting them, replaying them. But I had either such paltry dreams as to embarrass, or else these rare but sure visitations by a presence that seemed outside the possibility of dream. My mind spun, and a bitter taste formed in my mouth.

This was a morning when I questioned everything. The taste in my mouth thickened, as though I had sucked on a brass cartridge case all night, and when I tried to cut it with a swallow of brandy, I spit it out in disgust. I lay in the sleeping bag for another hour, watching false dawn tease the sky and then withdraw, then the true gray which signals day slowly seeped up from the east. As soon as I could see the outline of the eastern ridge, I arose, swiftly readied the pack, and headed off The Moon. All I knew is that I was heading back to Sterns, heading for some other travels, and I was impatient. Cerridwen could rot like her cat, if she were of the stuff which rots. If she weren't, let the void take her, or let my memory die.

CHAPTER 6

I CHOSE THE BROAD, southern-pointing ridge for my descent. It forms a heavy shoulder to The Moon and leads out into the desert beyond like an outstretched arm, some miles east of the cat's ridge and my own route of the past few days. It is rounded on the east, and sharp on the west, but the way is smooth, with only a few nicks and cuts to slow a fast return.

There is a distinct downhill art for the pedestrian which, mastered, saves legs from pounding under gravity's extra burden, and prevents the toes from wedging in the boots. It is a springy gait, with knees in front and ass slung back. Perhaps it looks a little silly, but it is simple, efficient, and fast. I wanted speed. My time on The Moon had not been as pleasant as I had come to expect, and I felt angry with myself, or my fate, or dreams, and the Hag, all in a jumble. My Eye had told me nothing from the night, blinded as it had been by the tumult of dreams. I did not know if anyone were following me or not, and did not care. I think if I had seen anyone that day or the next I would have killed him without hesitation, and with no more motive than irritation at his presence. It was because I had such feelings that I spent my life on The Moon, or something like her. I am not fit company for others, and know it. But now I was not fit for The Moon, either.

By late afternoon I had covered thirty miles and had descended to about seven thousand feet. The ridge ran another ten before it sunk into the desert. I had watered twice at springs and at the second killed a grouse with a well-hurled stone. I had gutted it quickly, and hung it on my pack for supper. I had neither seen nor felt the presence of another, though I had been careful to scan the ridge with my monocular whenever I stopped. Three miles beyond the second spring I came to a comma-shaped indentation in the ridge which covered about an acre. In one corner was a stand of Ponderosa pines, and I decided to camp there and cook the grouse. I built a fire, and as I waited for the coals, I made a quick grill on a Y-shaped branch from a small spool of wire from my pack. After several days on gruel, raisins, and a few dried apricots, it did not take much cooking to make the bird a feast. In the low light of dusk and my fire, I leaned back on my pack and savored the bird-flesh. The Moon's summit was hidden by the welling-up of the ridge and I would not see the peak for another day. That night I would sleep without dreaming, as though I had been given some reprieve for having left the heights.

I was on my way before dawn again, with ten

more miles of ridge to follow before I entered the desert. And before that, I planned to stop at the old mine. During my first year of walking The Moon I had come this way and found an abandoned mine tunnel in a side canyon. The mine was at least a hundred years old, and the tailings had so melded with the surface rock and been so overgrown that it was quite by accident that I had spotted the opening, hidden in a fold of the canyon wall. I don't believe anyone else had been there for many, many years. The mine was not large. A tunnel had followed a vein of ore in for perhaps a hundred feet, and then a stope had been worked, and three small tunnels driven in search of an orebody which must never have been found, or if found, had been a great disappointment. The west is full of such monuments. I liked the place because it was so difficult to find, and provided both shelter and safety. A few bats lived there, some harmless arachnids, and a family of venerable centipedes.

I quite remember the time, building fence, when a centipede had scurried from under a rock Uncle Angus had kicked aside, straight up his shin to his knee. It led to a classic leap, yelp, and pants-shedding, all somehow simultaneous. The creature had left a series of paired bites up his leg, a dozen or so, and Uncle Angus cursed for five minutes straight. The thought of Uncle Angus kept a smile on my face the last mile to the mine. He had been a good man, if careless about centipedes.

The Moon generally was conducive to such benign thoughts as the savory quality of grouse, and Uncle Angus's great yelp. It was a place where memory could be eased, or lulled, into pleasantries, and the raw horrors that had made up too much of life could be hidden by the very brightness of the day. And it was such a time I had on the descent, all the way to the old mine. I did not bother with the Hag or her stupid cat, or the wretched deceptions I had placated myself with over the years. Each step was an immediate history, complete in itself, as each glance to the side, each breath. I moved totally in the present, in the immediacy of a footfall. The Study Group was half a world away, and gone.

I took in the air of The Moon, her distances, the cloud-dark shadows of her canyons, the wheeling hawks, the stones and grass and brush, her trees, as few and hidden as her desert bighorns, and her solitude, most precious of all to me. I kept watch to my right, and soon came to the side canyon I must descend, a rough, big-bouldered rockfall most of the way, twisting back and forth on itself. There were two little water seeps in its length and near one I spooked three does. If I had been planning to stay longer I would have taken one. But the .270 stayed at my side as I watched them move nimbly and quickly up the steep slope. I watched them silently and admired the ultimate simplicity of a deer's mind. It was a machine much like the one that hummed between my own ears, but tuned to a Euclidean shyness, a world of coherent forms, or regularity, and it lacked ambiguity to the extent that it was fundamentally alien to human consciousness, awash in the stuff.

I had half begun a minor sermon on the subject when the tunnel opening appeared on the slope to my left. I scrambled up a hundred feet or so, watching the ground with more than common interest. I like to know if I am going to be someone's visitor or not. I saw no tracks, and the brush in front of the entrance was as thick and grasping—all cat's-claw and scrub oak—as ever. I sidled through the brush carefully, unhooking the cat's-claw from my trousers at each step. The air was still, and there was no sound in the canyon save my own step, and the rustle of brush against fabric. The morning sun was beginning to warm the air, and a trace of the dry dust inside the mine's entrance touched my nostrils. As I stepped into the entrance of the mine, the subtle shift in odor from outside air to something else came clearer, sharper to my nose. The air was cooler, and touched by the slight pungence of guano. It was the merest touch, and I wished for no more, as bats are notoriously rabid, and the virus of rabies can be transmitted by the air itself where there are numerous bats. Histoplasmosis, a fungus which feasts on the lungs, is another organism hosted by bats which I did not care to share. There was also the veriest touch of smoke in the air, and I hesitated as I first smelled it. Smoke there should not be. I did not like the smell of smoke, and slipped the rifle from my shoulder. I stopped and let my ears study the darkness within and my eyes studied the ground. My cache was undisturbed in the small alcove on the right. There were no footprints in the soft, fine dust a few feet within the opening. If something had made smoke, it was still inside, and had not come this way for many days. Or it was the damned Hag playing with molecules again. As my eyes gradually adjusted to the darkness, I walked slowly back into the tunnel. At just about the limit of vision, perhaps a hundred feet into the mountain, the entrance a blinding white dot behind my shoulder, and the blackness impenetrable beyond, I saw a small circle of stones on the tunnel's floor. There were a dozen stones a few inches apart in a circle surrounding the ivory white bones of a cat. The bones lay in precise anatomical order, like a museum specimen. I moved closer to the encircled skeleton and searched the dirt for prints. There were none. A few charred sticks were piled at six o'clock outside the circle, as though a tiny fire had been started and then snuffed out. The cat bones gleamed in the dim light, and seemed to have a luminescence of their own. Whatever it meant in the Hag's lore of symbols, it was clear no mortal had left such a funerary monument. As I knelt beside the ring I could see no dust on the bones. They were as clean as if they had just been licked. I picked up the skull and lower jaw and gazed a few moments into the empty eye sockets. It was a cat skull, no more. But since it had been put there expressly for me to see, I accepted it, and wrapped the skull and jaw carefully in my handkerchief. There might come a time when this cat's head would be worth the carriage. I picked up one of the charred sticks. It was piñon, with its characteristic aroma. It was cold, but still aromatic, and could not have been there more than a day or so at most. At least, I thought as I rose and turned toward the entrance, the Hag is willing to make signs in something of a stronger fabric than dreams. I was a little surprised at how calm I was.

I returned to my cache. About thirty feet from the entrance in an alcove once used to store tools was a shelf fixed to support timbers holding gallon tins, and from a nail hung a small day pack and a bota I had left there months ago. This was often a way station on my travels to The Moon. It was forty miles from here to Sterns, a nice day's run. I stashed my pack and gear here, and ran those miles in or out as mood and supplies directed. I had about fifty or sixty pounds of concentrated foods here—MPF soy protein, mashed potato flakes, powdered sugar, powdered milk, rice, oatmeal, dates, raisins, and dried apricots—dry and protected from mice and cats and such small deer by the gallon tins. I figured I had about a hundred thousand calories stored here, and that was enough to keep me fat and sassy for more than a month, and I could stretch the rations to three if I needed to.

On the shelf beside the tins were three bottles of Remy Martin, and a case of twenty-four cans of sliced pears. These were for my moments of excess or despair, or when the usually palatable taste of my gruel had become a source of existential anguish. A tot of cognac and a can of pears can ease the conscience of an Augustine brooding on imagined sins, or sate a womanless satyr. I took the flask from my pack, drained the last half ounce, and refilled it from one of the bottles. I would have a can of pears before I left. I checked the box. Eighteen remained.

It did not take long to strip off my clothes and boots, and slip on the Adidas racing flats from the day pack. I like to run naked, except for my feet. I rolled my shirt up and stuffed it into the big pack, unloaded the .270, and slipped my pants over the rifle as a makeshift dust jacket. I put the Palug cat's skull, his gold coins and currency in the day pack along with my pistol, the plastic water bottle, the silver brandy flask, and about a pound of sugar in a bag. I burn about four thousand calories in the six or so hours it takes for the run, and I seem to feel better when I take in about half that during the run. Not all runners tolerate sugar as well as I do, but it works for me. I keep a liter of fresh water in the bota, and a liter of sugared water in the bottle, and stop each hour to drink half a cup of the sugar water. There was a spring about a mile from the mine where I would fill bota and bottle, and two cattle tanks fifteen miles apart along the way. The only hard part was the first fifty yards through cat's-claw naked. After that the way opened up. Before I left I ate the pears.

Just beyond the spring where I took on water, the creek bed opened up to a broad avenue fit for a decent trot. I set myself to a nine minutes per mile pace and settled in. The great delight in running, to me, aside from the physical flush of controlled exertion, is a drifting-mindedness which permits me to focus on everything and nothing simultaneously. I have read it has something to do with the release of dopamine and other exotics by the brain, and well it may. Whatever, it is a tranquil state of psychic rest, and even at the end of a long run, when my body is aching with fatigue, my mind is as placid as a babe's.

The miles moved under my feet with stately dignity, the bota swung close to my lips every twenty minutes or so and I squirted a mouthful in. On the hour I paused to drink 50ml. of sugared water. By the end of the second hour I was near the first windmill and water tank. A few white-faced Herefords stood sullenly by the watering trough, wondering who they were and where. (Cattle are feeble-minded). The sun burned down amiably for a great distance, and I was as close to forgetting the Hag and her wretched cat as I had been in days, and was toying with the idea that I might go to Las Vegas to trade the gold coins for cash and move for a few hours myself in the sensual tawdriness of that place. With one of the Krugerrands I knew I could buy a most beautiful whore to do my bidding for an entire night. It had been long since I had indulged myself that way. I wasted the next few miles on puerile fantasies no worse than most amusements. The day was fresh, the breeze still carrying something of yesterday's rains, and the desert was as lovely as new skin. The frustrations and anger I had felt at The Moon's tip were gone now, and I was willing to be at peace with the Hag if she'd let me. I'd kill her cat again, of course. But she knew that.

At the second water tank, with only a dozen miles remaining before the luxury of my packing case at Sterns, I took off my shoes and pack and immersed myself in the trough. The same mud-minded Herefords looked on or beyond me with faint surprise, their cowy lives fit for no better than hamburger. The water was warm and silky and I was immensely refreshed by the bath. As I lay on my back in the water, stretching my toes and rubbing the salt from my head, I looked up into the Nevada sky. Two buzzards wheeled above the water hole, where all was still save for the creak of the windmill and my own quiet splashing. I had many times seen with such vulture's eyes, watching a creature I knew would be dead soon and unexpectedly. They could not chill me who called them brothers, though mine was the hand that felled what would be their food. I like those things attentive to death, and would have shot one of those stupid cows for them without a trace of regret except that the cows were not mine to shoot. Old Higgins' cows they were, a neighbor to Mary-Gail Henry, and friendly enough to me. Peace be with you, cows, I said as I tied my shoelaces and adjusted the pack. Peace, I said, and no more intelligence than you need. May you be tender and tasty and make Old Higgins rich.

The land between Old Higgins' water tank and Sterns sloped gently upward, enough to make the close of the run a challenge. Sterns lay on the western slope of a small mountain range which, like most in Nevada, ran north and south. Between it and the next small range, a southerly archipelago of The Moon, was a basin about forty miles across. The Moon lay north and west, and I was crossing the basin on the diagonal, south by east. The gas station Mary-Gail Henry ran was one of a cluster of four buildings that made up Sterns, and were all hers. The gas station, a separate building with customers' restrooms, her house adjacent, and her barn fifty yards distant. There were half a dozen cottonwoods that had survived the years since her first husband planted them a little after the Great War. Mary-Gail Henry was about seventy, had a daughter in her forties, and a granddaughter of twenty or so, the only other member of the family I had met. The daughter stayed in Las Vegas, but the granddaughter seemed to make regular visits. Four or five miles away I could see the bunching of objects which was trees and buildings. By three miles things were a bit more distinct, and I noticed a small column of smoke rising from the land behind the gas station, as though Gail were burning garbage. But it did not come from Gail's incinerator, it came from the general location of my packing case. I did not like the thought that arose in my mind.

I slowed my pace a bit, for I did not want to arrive at an emergency of some kind out of sorts. The closer I drew to Sterns, the surer I was that my packing case had been torched. Fire did not strike me as one of the Hag's weapons, and I began to think of the hundred other souls who might wish me dead if dismembered first. Enemies, friends of enemies, enemies of friends...sometime friends, disinterested bounty hunters, and any number of upholders of the most varied laws. I was guilty of capital crimes in twenty-three countries, and so I could nearly take my pick of punishments legally due: garrote, guillotine, poison gas, electricity, noose, firing squad, lethal injection, or battering by steel bar as in Uganda under Amin.

Two miles away I changed course slightly so I might make the last mile in the cover of the arroyo. I paused to take the SIG from the pack and check the magazine. I do this even when I am certain it is full. This was not the first time I had gone into action starkers, but it was not of my choosing this day. It was about four in the afternoon and there was enough shadow in the arroyo's bank to make me feel a little better. At a mile, I slowed to a walk and found a little cut in the bank where I could sit unobserved. I made up some sugar water and sipped it slowly while I rested. I took a nip or two of brandy as well. I gave myself fifteen minutes of tranquillity. My pulse was down to 65 or so, on its way to my resting 56, and the flush of running was gone. When I arose I slipped the pack and bota on one shoulder only, the easier to be free of them, and tried to forget that I had spent the last six hours running forty miles and had a perfect right to be a bit tuckered out. I was able to get a good view of my little homestead while remaining well hidden by the bank of the arroyo. There was no doubt it was my packing case smoldering there. I could only hope whoever had done it had stolen the rifles and particularly my old 1911. I did not want to lose that one in a fire. Stolen, I might well recover them, but burnt and all the temper in the steel destroyed, I would be out some decent memories and trusted machines.

Gail Henry's pickup truck was parked beside the garage. There was a red Toyota there I had seen before. It belonged to her granddaughter. And there was a dark blue Ford LT parked by the pumps. The yellow glint on the bumper made it from California. I moved over to a blind approach and moved swiftly across the remaining three hundred yards. Any sight of me would be blocked by the restroom building. I pressed against its wall and listened—first for the sound of anyone in the restrooms, and then for any sound at all. It was quiet. And then I heard the screen door of the station squeak open and slam shut, and the crunch of a man's footsteps in the gravel. As the steps approached the restrooms, I heard a scream from the gas station. It sounded like Gail Henry's granddaughter's voice.

The steps continued and I heard the door of the restroom open and close. There was the soft sound of a zipper, a sigh, and a healthy stream of piss into the bowl. The woman screamed again and I considered my method. The kindling pile was a few feet away, and I saw a yard-long piece of baling wire on the ground. In one step I had the wire and two small pieces of wood, and quickly twisted the ends of the wire on the handles. It wasn't the piano wire I usually employed, but 'twould do. I stood behind the door, and when it opened, slipped the wire over his head to his throat, hauled back, pivoted 180 degrees, the wire twisted, and I bent forward swiftly, taking his weight on my hips as I pulled him back up. The garrote is soundless, and no scream is possible, but it does not kill by strangulation: the wire cuts deeply into the neck and severs the carotid artery along with the windpipe, and a great geyser of blood shoots into the air. We were both drenched, and he was dead in seconds. I let him fall to the ground, wiped his blood from my face, and glanced at the back door of the service station. No one was there, but there was another scream. At his waist I found a 9mm Tokarev, which made it likely I was dealing with one of the boys from Mokryye Dela, "the department of wet affairs," once again. They were the KGB assassins, colleagues of a sort.

I shifted the SIG to my left hand, and took his piece in my right after checking to see that a round was in the chamber. There would not be more than three in the station. One was amusing himself with the woman, and the other two were doubtless watching. I glanced down at my blood-covered body and decided the proper tactic was swift assault. I sprinted to the station door, opened it enough — both spatially and temporally — to see Gail Henry lying on the floor, apparently dead, two men at the counter, beers in hand, watching a third man fuck and beat a woman on the floor.

I double-tapped each one at the counter with the 9mm, and as the man on the floor rolled off the girl and tried to scramble to his feet, I shot him three times in the lower abdomen with the Tokarev. One shot seemed to strike his penis, and he clutched himself and began to roll and scream. The woman looked at me and screamed again. "Be quiet," I shouted, and both hushed for a moment. "Lady, you are Okay. No one will hurt you now." I tried to be placating and believable, but she was deep in fear and shock. "You, tovarich," and I spoke slowly in Russian, "keep your hands on your balls." He rolled his eyes, groaned, and held his seeping groin, knowing he was dead. "Why did you burn my box?" I asked. "What did you expect to find?" His glare was stony, but lost, and I knew in his mind he was remembering a wife, a mistress, a child, a dacha, a motorbike, perhaps the cow on the collective farm that kicked him when he was eight and determined his future. I shot him in the head twice.

The other two were as dead as I expected them to be, but I gathered their pistols anyway. Then I turned to the woman. "I am William Gasper," I told her. "I live here sometimes. Gail Henry was my friend." She nodded dumbly. "We are both bloody," I said, holding out my arms. "You go to the bathroom and clean up. I will clean up at the sink behind the bar." She nodded, and began to get to her feet. I did not help her, but kept my distance, thinking she would not want another strange man's touch just now, even in aid. She stumbled to the bathroom in the living quarters off the barroom-cum-office and cafe. I walked to the corpse of Gail Henry and saw that she had not been killed kindly. Perhaps I should have let him sit gut-shot a little longer. I heard the shower start, and I went to the sink.

I got my shirt from my pack, but my extra pants had been burned in my box, so I pulled a pair off the corpse that seemed closest to me in size, hoping death had not relaxed his sphincters totally just yet. They had a few bloody spots, but were free of shit. "Small graces," I said to myself, "make the day." In a while I opened a beer and sat down. The woman came out, her wet hair brushed, dressed in a shirt and Levi's, and running shoes. I had wrapped Gail Henry's body in a blanket, and put it on the bar. I had dragged the men's corpses out the back door, put them on the kindling pile. But I was too tired to mop the floor.

The woman's face was bruised, and her hand shook slightly as I handed her a glass of whiskey. "They send two teams. I don't think we ought to wait around for the police or anything. The second team checks on the first team. Makes sure the job was done, and discourages defections." She seemed to understand. "Get some clothes, a quilt or something, some food. I'll check their car."

I went outside, got a gallon can, and went to the kerosene pump. I covered the four men with kindling, and log butts from the wood stack, and started a good fire with the kerosene. They wouldn't disappear, but identification would take time, if KGB boys can ever be identified here. The car was rented in Las Vegas, and there were four Uzis and twenty loaded magazines in a suitcase in the trunk. I put two of the Uzis and ten of the magazines on the front seat beside me. I had put their Makarovs and Tokarevs, wallets, extra magazines, keys, and small change in a paper bag. I went inside and got a case of beer and three bottles of whiskey from the bar, and filled another sack with lunch meat and bread. Gail Henry drank bottled water instead of her well's alkali, and so I put ten gallons in the trunk. There was nothing of my own to bring except the pack, and the loot of The Moon.

The woman came out, her arms filled with a quilt and pillow. "Get in the back seat. You should try to sleep," and then I asked, "Are you hurt inside? Are you bleeding? Do you have any medicines?" She didn't nod, and I helped her into the back seat. "Lie down, I'm just about ready." I went back inside and took the display box of painkillers and hangover remedies from the bar. We both might need these later. The fire in the woodpile was going well as I headed the Ford south on the highway. I actually knew where I was going.

CHAPTER 7

THERE IS A very secondary road that runs
west of the Pancake Range down to Warm
Springs, a hundred or so miles away. There
I'd have to jog a few miles on Highway 25 before
I could start my route east in a mesh, a weave of
roads, some paved, some not, and none patrolled.
It did not seem likely the KGB or the Company
could possibly cover this route. I would drive into
the night, and toward the dawn, and meet sunrise
in the Escalante desert outside Cedar City. I had
some options in Cedar City, and would use the
drive to sort them out.

The Ford ballooned along in some tentative
float, but as long as I backed off on the curves, it
could keep 90 or so on the straightaways. When
I glanced in the rearview mirror at the woman,
I half expected to see Cerridwen sitting there,
a sardonic smile on her face, but it was just the
woman sleeping, the quilt pulled over her shoulders
protectively. I had been raped once, in prison, and
knew something of the content of her dreams. I
wished her sleep. The Pancakes loomed dark on

the east horizon and then the rising moon began to lighten the sky. Cerridwen would be riding that, I mused, stitching a new skin for her Palug cat. I decided I had a right to feel sorely afflicted—by a demon thing out of the remainder, and by agents of the earth's own dark. KGB teams do not operate without the Company knowing. Sometimes I think there is tacit agreement between them, and in my case I could well imagine some coordination to rid the world of William Gasper, for whatever embarrassment he might provide in the mythical future. My annuities were not in the form of a government check, green in the mail, but assured by banks in Switzerland, Hong Kong, Berlin, London, Singapore, and Sydney. I had bank boxes in Portugal, Israel, South Africa, and Stockholm as well, stuffed with gelt, not paper. They could not touch my income, and they knew it. They did not care a whit. But they could—and apparently had—ordered me dead. Why? If there were a God, even He would not know.

I had seen no lights, or other cars, since we left Gail Henry's place. But I knew my adversaries could well have planted a transmitter on the Ford, and were kept appraised of my location by satellite. It is easily done, and I had not the time to check out the car thoroughly. But this did not concern me greatly. In Warm Springs I would send this Ford on to Las Vegas, and transfer to my old truck, stored in Elmer's Garage there. Elmer's boy would love to make $300 to drive to Vegas, especially on a Friday.

We were there in less than an hour and a half. I parked beside my old pickup, and helped the woman, still groggy with sleep, into the bunk in the camper. I gave Elmer's son the three hundred, grinned back at his toothy grin, and told him to park the Ford in some casino's parking lot, and never go back to it. I always top the tank when I park the old Power Wagon, and so was on my way in less than ten minutes. The next few hours involved following a cobweb of ranch roads and county routes east, over the Utah border, and on to peaceful Cedar City. If you can blend in, Utah offers wonderful concealment. I had spent long months in Utah towns, attending Ward Meetings, establishing my bona fides as Brother William Gasper, or some other name, a Saint of Deseret, returned to Zion after years abroad in business. I knew Bishops of a dozen Stakes, and could provide references that were less fanciful than one might expect. I knew a place in Cedar City where the woman would be safe until she decided to move on.

The way there was always easterly, but not direct. I went by Adaven, Ursine, Beryl, and Iron Springs, and the woman slept. The moon was in my face for some time, but gradually rode high above me, and out of sight. You may wonder why the woman is in the story, hardly speaking, hardly more than a prop. Should we fall in love? Should we banter? Should I take her to her door? What false scenarios our entertainments suggest! I know hurt, and I know grief, having been the cause of much myself. There is nothing binding or erotic in shared sorrow, in panic, in dreadful action. I knew her name once, was introduced to her. But I cannot remember her name, only that she was Gail Henry's grandchild. I would not ask her name when I left her in Cedar City. If this is a story, it is not a romance, unless Cerridwen's doting attention could be so construed. It is, as far as the teller knows, a veritable account of a lucid insanity of long duration, an oblique confession, an apologia pro vita sua, a fantasy spun in a cold winter, or out of night.

Here on the porch of the Ranch on the River Sorrow, where I type these words on an old Royal 440, and I can glance through cottonwoods to the dun yellow red-streaked cliffs that rise above the Sorrow, I cannot tell you where the woman is, or who buried Gail Henry, or who else will search for William Gasper. I remember Archimedes Pati, the American who delivered Viet Nam to Uncle Ho in 1945, in a long coordination with the Other, directed by Washington and Moscow. I have drunk all night with those who knew the Emperors never have new clothing, and who pay the tailors. Shadows are the real business of the world, shadows. Ernst Jünger wrote that soldiers are "workers in the lethal realm," *Arbeiter im tödlichen Raum*, and in those terms I have been a soldier long. A cat skull sits on the desk beside the Royal and my favorite pistol beside that. Both are for Cerridwen. Each one an illusion to fight an illusion. There is a rock beside the river I sit on to await the moon, and I have had famous thoughts there, famous and evanescent. I am at one hundred and forty now, and not tired of it, yet—not even in the minor leagues of death. Negligible, without the temperament to be a great killer. I debate my sanity with the River Sorrow, but it does not reply. The cottonwoods regard me as though I were innocent and virgin. The birds sing to me as easily as they sang to Job, or Christ, or Napoleon. There is nothing I can do which either offends or pleases the universe. And I am no different from you.

It does not snow here often, and if it does, I do not expect to see a new column mount on the air, ice crystals glinting like tiny swords, and the cloud roaring beyond mere wind's possibilities. I would no more see that than I would Chinese armies pouring down the canyon. The past is real only in memory, and memory is a small electric current, more fragile than a spider's web.

These memoirs I offer for their curiosity, for I know of no others—so peculiar. There are few skills I possess which have not elsewhere been more carefully presented. Many a greater sniper has detailed the art, and what could I say of hunting that Ortega y Gasset has not plumbed more gracefully? Of stealth, of trekking, of long, silent marches . . . this is most of human history. But I was chosen by The Moon. Now this is strange. Even if it is mad, it is strange. Cerridwen weaves a web of silver in the sky, brilliant as the egg sack of a spider which feeds on light, and she slips down on her silk wherever The Moon shines. She slips through the trees, through glass, wherever the silken light flows, and she is certainly as real as light, and more, for I have felt her body, seen her clothed and naked, even, for an instant, felt her cover me like a sheath before she turned to wind and was away. Old or young, her face is a long study at the edge of beauty and beyond, and her eyes are terror and promise at once.

I have tried to think that she is some aspect of myself, something unresolved, some conundrum come with birth. But she is no more I than you are. And she will boil up out of the water of the Sorrow in some fierce leap marked by The Moon's track, and take all I know away. Physics tells us we are all starlight, cycled energies manifested this way once, and then another. We are all light, in our heavy meat and throbbing blood. Our aches are light, our bones, our sparkling shit, our fevers and our dreams, all light.

HOWARD MCCORD

*is the author of more than thirty
books of poetry, fiction, criticism, and
travel writing. He has walked extensively
in Iceland, Lapland, Greece, India, Alaska,
and Southeast Asia. His walk of the Jornada
del Muerto in New Mexico is the subject of a
forthcoming book. He is a veteran of the Korean
War and forty-three years of university teaching,
many of those as Director of the Creative Writing
Program at Bowling Green State University.
He has run twelve marathons, and at age forty-nine
completed a sixty kilometer ultra-marathon in 6:53:06.
He has written extensively for the firearms press and
won the Bob Loveless Award in 1996 for the best
article in* GUN DIGEST. *An NRA Certified
Pistol Instructor, he has taught the
Concealed Handgun Carry course
offered by BGSU. Among his fellowships
and awards are a Woodrow Wilson National
Fellowship, a Fulbright to India, the D. H. Lawrence
Fellowship of the University of New Mexico, and two
National Endowment for the Arts fellowships
—one for this book.*